about the book

PEN AND PERIL

**Mystery meets romantic comedy
in the Comet Cove Mysteries!**

A new job. A new romance. A new ... murder?

Reporter Roz Melander has juggled more than enough chaos since she moved back to her quirky Florida hometown. After breaking the big story that led her to the reinvented *Courier-Beacon*, she has her hands full with work ... and a hot-off-the-press romance with colleague Alden Knox. But when they stumble upon a disturbing death that looks like murder, she knows they have another explosive story to investigate.

Alden's specialty is digging up celebrity dirt, but he'd rather not go through a grave to do it. The hapless movie producer who was killed behind Comet Cove's bookstore—in the middle of a signing by Alden's favorite author—had glittering connections and a gift for gab. It seems everyone at the event knew him. But who wanted him dead?

As Roz and Alden chase leads, secrets, and a decent cup of coffee through their star-studded beach town, their story takes a treacherous turn. Can they unravel the mystery before someone else dies—or, perish the thought, they miss deadline?

Pen and Peril is a low-spice funny romantic mystery. This novel contains mild cursing, unabashed longing and closed-door canoodling with lots of giggles. This is the second book in the Comet Cove Mysteries by Lucy Lakestone, author of the Bohemia Bartenders Mysteries.

Pen and Peril

Comet Cove Mysteries
Book Two

LUCY LAKESTONE

Velvet Petal Press
Florida

for the truth-tellers

Map of Comet Cove, Florida

Fanciful and not to scale

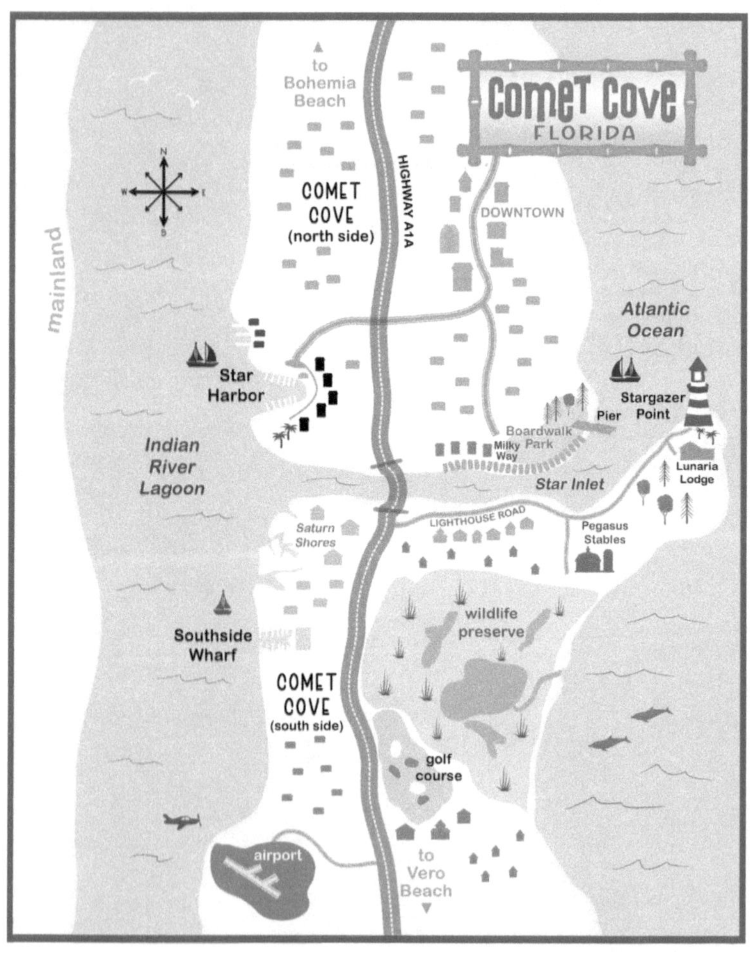

chapter
one

Once upon a time in Florida

"ROZ, sweetheart, the beauty of writing fiction is that you can make up anything you want," Alden told her. He took a sip of his coffee as they walked along Comet Cove's busy Main Street toward Big Bang Books. "It's pure imagination. Novels exist at a higher level than our scribbling for the newspaper."

Roz shot him a skeptical look, but it turned into a smile. How did she end up with a guy this good-looking? Muscular but not one of those big doofuses who lived at the gym, he was even more attractive when he was relaxed like he was now, in jeans and a button-up blue shirt, sleeves rolled up, on the way to see his favorite author.

She was skeptical about Alden's claim about the superiority of fiction. She was skeptical about the book signing they were about to attend. And she wasn't sure about him calling her sweetheart, either. Having a serious boyfriend—man friend?—was pretty new to her. So was just about everything in her life, since *The Beacon* gobbled up her family's newspaper and the staffs merged.

And she and Alden had merged, too. Though it wasn't exactly a perfect union yet.

"What are you smiling at?" he asked, his gray eyes narrowing.

Roz tasted her mocha, sweet and hot from Bean Me Up, and quoted him. *"Our scribbling for the newspaper?* Are you saying what you wrote for the tabloids wasn't fiction?"

"Now that's a low blow. I reported the facts—in a colorful way. Besides, I'm a reformed character, and that was a long time ago." He shot her a grin and ran a hand through his thick, short-cropped hair.

"Not all that long ago," she said, enjoying his humor. And his hair. Hers had more reddish tones than his dark brown. "And have you made any progress on *your* novel?"

"I'm still working on the outline," he confessed.

"I think you're afraid to start it."

"Not fair! I'm busy, that's all. I've got this crazy job covering all the celebrities hanging out in Comet Cove. If only I had help from our new managing editor-slash-star reporter, maybe I'd have more time for fiction."

"Ha! I'm busy too, you know. This place is growing. There's lots to write about."

"Because with growth comes growing pains."

"Too true," Roz agreed. "It's nothing like it was when I was a kid."

She cast a look around the cute downtown, filled with colorful small businesses, the sidewalk dappled with shadows from palms and oak trees. It was April and cool for Florida, but she could feel summer waiting in the dressing room, trying on bathing suits. It was the end of what most Floridians called

The Season, the busy time when snowbirds came to stay, but on both sides of the street, almost every diagonal parking space was full.

This place was thriving thanks to all the people moving in, but how long would it have that sleepy small-town charm she'd grown up with? When she'd gone off to college and later even farther away to work at a Baltimore paper, Comet Cove had been so sleepy it was practically falling into a coma. Then a few famous people found it, and somehow its appeal exploded like a supernova. She was always tripping over celebrities in unexpected places.

And now they were going to see one of them at Big Bang Books.

"So have you read a lot of Enolia Honeywood's novels?" she asked Alden. "I didn't think sexy beach thrillers were your kind of thing."

"Why not? I'm sexy and thrilling, aren't I?"

She laughed, though he really was. Even if she was freaking out a little bit about being in a relationship after their whirlwind romance, which happened to coincide with reporting on a big story they'd barely survived.

Alden chuckled, too. "Seriously, she's the best. A master of the craft. Her twists get me every time. I'd love to write half that well."

"Or make half as much as she does," Roz said wryly.

"I won't deny it. But I guess I should write my novel first."

"I'm a little surprised she's making this appearance," she said. "There's a much bigger bookstore in Vero Beach she could've gone to."

"You're right. She usually picks big cities for her appearances these days. I think the only reason she's here is because she just bought a house on the beach on the north side."

Everything in Comet Cove was northside or southside, depending on which side of the inlet it was on. The inlet was the waterway that cut through the barrier island from the Indian River Lagoon to the Atlantic, making this a popular place for boaters and anglers as well as the glitterati.

They'd almost reached Big Bang Books, where fans of Enolia Honeywood streamed inside. The storefront was on theme, painted with planets, stars and flying books. Big picture windows flanked the blue door, which was spangled with silver stars.

The window display on one side offered an array of Ms. Honeywood's bestsellers, surrounded by beach trappings—flip-flops, an umbrella, a beach towel, shells. Oh, and a scary-looking knife sticking out of a sand-filled bucket, which Roz hoped was a rubber prop.

The window on the other side was full of science fiction and comic books, which were among Big Bang's specialties. It also carried plenty of romance, bestsellers, quirky reads, kids' fare and banned books. There was something for everyone inside.

Alden held the door for her, and she strolled into the frosty air-conditioning. He briefly caressed her back as they paused at the entrance, then stuck his hands in his pockets as he gazed around at the crowd.

She loved his touch, but getting smoochy in public probably didn't do much for their reputations as journalists with *The Courier-Beacon,* so they tried to keep PDAs to a minimum. All part of adjusting to the whole relationship thing. This wasn't Roz's first, but it was so much *more.* She'd never been so emotionally entangled with a guy before. And now she was all mixed up.

Big Bang Books wasn't chain-store large, but it was

spacious. It had taken over an old shoe store that had been half a dozen other things over the years. It had that lovely bookish smell of paper and ink and binding glue.

Under high tin ceilings, dozens of people milled among the bookshelves or claimed seats in the rows of chairs set up in the back. Their voices echoed and overlapped in a roaring waterfall of words. Kids giggled and screeched in the children's section. A local folk duo played guitar and flute in one corner. This was no bookishly quiet event. It was a party, and it was loud.

"Should we get a seat before they run out?" Alden's voice held a touch of boyish anxiety that made Roz smile.

"Maybe we should mingle first."

"You're just looking for a story."

"And you aren't?" She quirked her mouth at him. "Maybe I just want to say hi to my friends."

"Ha. Fine. I think I see a likely target anyway." He glanced to the right, toward a few men clustered around the history section.

"Is that—*that guy?*" Roz asked. "Blake Burbage, right?" He was fiftysomething and handsome in a silver fox kind of way, his dark hair threaded with steel-gray and his blue eyes sharp and dancing as he laughed with his cohorts.

"Yep. Blake Burbage. I haven't seen him in anything good in forever."

"I loved him in that show about the Army police—*Chain of Honor*. And then he played that officer in ... I can't remember."

"Probably because he's played a military man in so many movies and shows," said Alden, an avid film fan. "He hasn't had a big role in ten years. Though he did play that crazed priest in *Say a Hail Mary*."

"Oh, yeah!" Roz exclaimed. "He was super creepy in that one."

"He's still too famous to be a has-been. I'll see if I can chat him up." And off Alden went to do what he did best, mine the stars for gold.

Roz went the other way, spotting someone a lot less famous flipping through a tome on a display table covered with dragon books and merchandise. "Sheryl?"

The woman was slender with highlighted shoulder-length brown hair. She wore a brown T-shirt that said *Trees Hug Me Back* that hung straight down over her modest chest and bunched around the waistband of her tan capris. Thick leather sandals and a patchwork, cross-body boho bag completed the look.

One of the paper's stable of poorly paid freelancers, Sheryl Pugh wrote the gardening column. Not that the poor pay bothered her that much. She'd apparently survived a bitter divorce from a philandering Bohemia Beach allergist, emerging with enough money to pick and choose her careers, no matter how little they paid.

"Hey, Roz!" A smile lit up Sheryl's pretty elfin face, subtly tan and only slightly weathered by sun and her fortysomething years. "Are you a fan of Enolia Honeywood too?"

Roz got close enough to whisper. "Don't tell anyone, but I've only read one of her books, and it wasn't my favorite. Is she here yet?"

"I think she's hiding in the office. Or maybe she's coming by limo. No one seems to know, but there's a podium and table set up in front of the chairs, so I think she'll be here." Sheryl bore a small frown at the thought of being stood up.

"I'm sure she will. What are you writing about this week?"

Sheryl's brown eyes sparkled. "Plumeria! They're already

starting to leaf out. Soon they'll be blooming. It's always an exciting time, especially since they're just a bunch of fat sticks during the winter. And they smell so good."

"Great!" Roz tried to muster convincing enthusiasm. "Are those the flowers they have in Hawaii?"

"Yes, but they thrive here as well. Frangipani. I love them."

"I grew up here, but I never learned much about gardening. As a kid I didn't care, and as a grown-up, I'm just too busy."

"Roz." Sheryl closed the book she'd been riffling through and gave her a serious look. "Gardening is the best therapy ever. I mean, outside of sex."

Roz barked out a laugh at Sheryl's unexpected declaration. Sheryl grinned, then her eyes brightened again as she spotted someone enter the shop with another jingle of the door.

The man was exceptionally tan, probably artificially so when Roz compared him with Sheryl. He had a long, slender nose and distinct cheekbones, and his perfect teeth matched the white open-collar shirt he wore under an expensive-looking umber sport coat over slouchy khakis. His posh brown leather sneakers probably cost as much as all of Roz's shoes put together. His brown hair just brushed his shoulders, a bit wavy. He was polished in a way few locals were, but if he was famous, Roz didn't recognize him.

"Wayne!" Sheryl called out.

The man grinned and walked over, kissing Sheryl on both cheeks. French, Hollywood, pretentious, or all three, Roz judged.

He took both of Sheryl's hands. "You look wonderful, darling. Has she arrived yet?"

"We think she's hiding." Sheryl wore a bashful expression as he released her.

Wayne had turned toward Roz at the mention of "we."

"Wayne Vandershell." He held out his hand, and she shook it. His grip was firm and deliberate as he subtly scanned her budget casual outfit of jeans and a green knit shirt. His smile never faltered. "And you are?"

"Roz Melander." She didn't see a need to mention her job at the paper yet. After all, theoretically, she had the day off.

"Roz. I'm delighted to meet you."

Roz, always a little guarded around new people, found herself thawing under the warmth of his charm. Maybe his enthusiasm wasn't an act, even if his tan was.

"Roz is a brilliant writer." Sheryl gave him a meaningful glance, and Wayne's eyes widened.

"Is that right?" he asked. "What do you write?"

"Scintillating summaries of city council meetings, mostly," Roz replied. "I work for *The Courier-Beacon*."

Wayne blinked. "Really? No novels or screenplays in the offing like Sheryl here?"

Roz couldn't help chuckling. "Fiction's not my passion." But Sheryl? That was interesting. "You might want to talk to my colleague Alden. He's the one with all the imaginative ideas."

"You'll have to introduce me." Wayne scanned the room, then looked at Sheryl. "I need to make the rounds, my love, and have a quick smoke. And, of course, I need to talk to Enolia." He winked. "Save me a seat."

"Will do." Sheryl, the steady woman of the outdoors, fluttered her eyelashes like a debutante at her first ball as Wayne scurried off.

"So, Wayne, huh?" Roz asked.

Sheryl ran her finger over the shiny cover of the book she'd been perusing earlier, tracing the outline of a sword surrounded by roses. "He's nice. He wants to make my screenplay into a movie."

Now Roz really was surprised. She'd edited Sheryl's columns on occasion. Her facts were outstanding. The prose? Not so much. She must rock at dialogue. "That's pretty amazing. Is he a director?"

"Producer. He's putting down roots here. Listen, I'd better go get our seats."

"No problem. Have fun," Roz said.

She looked around, spotting dark-haired Liani Reyes, who ran Lunaria Lodge with her husband, and strawberry-blond April Reins, who owned a horse stable on the south side of town. And yes, April's career was proof that naming was destiny. Or perhaps she adopted her moniker back when she used to do horse stunts for a traveling circus.

They were chatting with a harried-looking blond woman in her mid-thirties who held a toddler and kept half an eye on two kids in the children's section. The little boy and girl had used a scarf to tie a stuffed Winnie-the-Pooh to a chair and were subjecting the bear to an intense interrogation.

Roz snorted and walked over to say hi to the grown-ups.

After the hellos, Liani did the honors. "Roz, this is Nicole Esquivel. You may have run into her husband, Sebastian?"

She'd certainly heard of him. Sebastian was a land developer and part of the Esquivel family, which mostly kept to itself. It also controlled a lot of land here in Mosquito County and had donated a huge tract to Comet Cove that was now a wildlife refuge.

"It's great to meet you," Roz said. "Are you a big fan?"

"I love Enolia Honeywood's books! Sometimes they're all that keep me sane. Mateo!" Nicole called out. "You and Gabriela untie that bear!" She turned back to the women. "Sorry I'm so distracted. I couldn't get a sitter, and I really wanted to be here. Though my husband should've picked them up by now."

"No problem." April seemed amused.

"And who's this little guy?" Roz asked of the munchkin in Nicole's arms, who drooled as he chewed on a *Guardians of the Galaxy* action figure.

"I am Groot!" the toddler said.

"Diego!" Nicole corrected him. "He's obsessed with Groot." And found Groot tasty, given who he was chewing on.

"Nice name," Liani said. "Diego, I mean."

Nicole nodded. "Sebastian wanted to name him after his father, who died when Seb was a boy."

"Aw, that's sweet," said April.

Liani looked wistful. "I remember when my boy was that age. It's a precious time. It won't be long before you'll be paying their way through college and watching them get their first jobs."

Nicole's stricken look was almost comical. The idea of raising kids to adulthood must be overwhelming no matter where you were in the process. Roz didn't know if she had the fortitude. She couldn't imagine motherhood anytime soon, and baby showers gave her hives. Maybe they just reminded her of everything she'd put off in favor of chasing the news.

She was saved from talking by a voice shouting from the back of the room.

"Ladies and gentlemen, please take your seats!" the woman by the podium called. "We'll start in just a few minutes!"

The audience scurried for the few remaining folding chairs. April and Liani smiled at each other and dashed toward the seats.

Nicole took a detour to tell her two older kids to stay quiet and leave Pooh alone.

"But I have to pee!" Mateo whined.

"Oh, all right. I'll take you. Gabriela, be good and stay right there. Ms. Roz is watching you."

Roz raised an eyebrow. Gabriela gave her a suspicious once-over and exclaimed, "I'm going with you, Mommy."

Nicole shrugged at Roz and dragged her three-child circus to the back hallway.

Everyone's a critic, Roz thought.

The podium was empty again, and the musicians started playing another song, so she took a moment to look over the new hot romances. She might not write fiction, but she loved reading it. Sometimes she needed an escape from the facts, especially when they were too grim.

A few minutes later, the woman at the podium had returned: Mae Middleton, proprietor of Big Bang Books. She wore a flowing dress covered in moons and stars, and her purple-streaked black hair was piled high on her head. Heavy eyeliner, silver jewelry and a galaxy of tattoos on her pale skin added to the fortune-teller vibe.

Roz liked her look, and she liked Mae, a sweet person she remembered from her days at Comet Cove High. Mae had been a year behind her in school. Roz was thirty-two, but she had to admit the curvy Mae looked a lot younger. Especially when she beamed as she was doing now.

"It's great to see so many people here!" Mae clasped her hands together, as giddy as a kid at a carnival. "Are you all as excited as I am?"

The crowd cheered, and Mae paused as a pale, balding man in a bow tie and spectacles walked up and spoke in her ear.

Roz looked around for Alden. He was on the other side of the room, but he glanced up to catch her eye. Almost all the chairs were full, though one remained next to Sheryl, and several people stood among the shelves next to the event space. Many clutched freshly purchased copies of Enolia's latest novel, *The Murex Murder*.

Mae nodded to bow-tie guy, who vanished into the back hallway, crossing paths with Blake Burbage, who emerged and slipped off to the side. The bathrooms back there were probably getting a lot of use, given the free beverages a young woman in red-framed eyeglasses poured at the refreshment table. Roz tossed her empty coffee cup in a waste can, quietly accepted a flute of champagne from the bookseller, and turned her attention to Mae.

"To all of you who preordered a copy of Enolia's new novel, thank you for keeping the lights on!" Mae said to a round of laughter. "Just show Enolia your golden special-edition bookmark so she knows you actually paid for it"—more titters—"and she'll be glad to sign your book after she chats with us for a bit. We have a few more copies in case you haven't picked one up yet. So ... are you ready?"

As the fans clapped in anticipation, Mae pulled her phone from a hidden pocket, tapped the screen and started reading. "Enolia Honeywood is an international bestselling author of more than fifty books, and she's synonymous with the term 'beach read.' Her success began with the thriller *Shellbreak Island,* which, just between us, I hear is soon to become a major motion picture." The room buzzed.

"In the past thirty years, she's hit No. 1 on the *New York Times* bestseller list a dozen times. She's currently single—take note, gentlemen!" A ripple of amusement passed through the crowd as Roz wondered what "currently" implied. "And she's just moved into our very own Comet Cove. And now, with no further ado, I'd like to introduce our honored guest and my favorite author of all time, Enolia Honeywood!"

chapter
two

ALDEN, who'd opted not to grab a chair given his good view from the sidelines, was torn between the thrill of seeing his favorite author emerge from the dark back hallway and his twinge of jealousy at seeing Roz talking to that slick dude with the long hair and radioactive smile. Who was that guy?

Of course, Alden had been busy, too, trying to warm up Blake Burbage. The actor hadn't shooed him off, probably a sign of just how far he'd fallen. Or maybe Alden was just good at small talk, at making people laugh and feel comfortable. It was a skill that served him well when he worked for the *National Eye*, and he used it often as a social and features writer now. He was uniquely placed in Comet Cove to cover its oddly burgeoning celebrity scene, and the fact that he liked the small-town, beachy lifestyle—and had met Roz—made his situation almost perfect.

Except that he worried Roz was nervous about their very new relationship. It hadn't helped that merging their two publications had been stressful and intense, even if everyone who wanted a job still had one. Then Alden had impulsively confessed his love for her after the big story that made national headlines. He knew she cared for him. But he also knew he could be about as subtle as a steamroller, and the truth was, having all the feels was pretty new for him, too.

They'd work it out. They had to. Because he couldn't imagine it any other way.

Blake had gone to the head, then relocated when he came out. So Alden drifted toward Roz, who now stood by a refreshment table to the left of the audience. Almost fifty fans, he guessed. They stood and clapped and shouted at the arrival of the dramatic Dame Enolia Honeywood.

OK, she wasn't a Dame, as far as he knew. But she should've been. Especially in that flowing dress—not unlike Mae's, except Enolia's was splashed with a tropical floral print. Big jewelry, silver-blond hair, emphatic pink makeup and probably a little surgical touch-up gave her a polished look.

He knew she was in her sixties. She could've passed for a decade younger at least. She wasn't a beautiful woman, but she was attractively confident. She didn't seem like someone trying too hard to be famous for social media. She didn't need to. She had beach pails full of charisma out of the gate.

"Hello, my dears!" she called out, waving around a shiny jacketed hardcover of her book. "Craig here is going to give you all a special memento of this occasion as I talk. Just be patient, and everyone will get one."

The crowd murmured in excitement as the fortyish balding man in the bow tie and wire-rimmed eyeglasses who'd followed her out of the hallway—seriously, a nerd right out of Central Casting—smiled nervously and shifted the open box he carried onto one arm. He moved toward the crowd and began handing out cellophane-wrapped rectangular objects sealed with red curly ribbons. It took a moment for Alden to realize they were thick sugar cookies decorated with the cover of Enolia's novel.

Alden had reached Roz by now and bent over to whisper in her ear. "A generous gesture," he said.

"She can afford it," Roz murmured back. She offered him a half-full glass of champagne, and he took it gladly, quaffing a refreshing sip of cool bubbles. It wasn't high quality, but even mediocre champagne had its appeal. Especially since he'd finished his coffee ages ago. Caffeine, meet alcohol. Shall we dance?

"All right, settle down. I'm going to tell you a story," Enolia called out, ignoring the podium as she paced in front of the audience.

A flash made Alden jump. He turned to see their staff photographer, Hai Yung, shooting photos with his big camera.

"No flash, please," Craig declared.

"It's fine, Craig. You may take a few photos with the flash," Enolia called out to Hai, whose superpower was being invisible in most situations. It was how he got such great photos.

"I don't have to, ma'am," the twentysomething photographer replied, looking embarrassed.

"Please," the author said. "You don't mind, do you, my friends?"

The crowd laughed, some said no, and with the slightest cringe, Hai shot a few more photos of Enolia in various theatrical poses, holding up her book each time. Then he ostentatiously popped the flash off the camera, stowed it in his backpack and retreated between two rows of bookshelves.

Enolia nodded, an amused smile on her face. Clearly, she wanted to milk the photo op. But she was cheeky enough to tweak the nose of the press while she was doing it.

Alden spotted freelancer Sheryl Pugh as she stood, looked around, then scurried out of her row, around the crowd and Enolia, and toward the back hallway. Restroom, he guessed.

Enolia watched her go. "Was it something I said?"

Laughter followed. A disheveled woman with three kids came out of the hallway, looking frustrated. "Get that lovely woman a glass of champagne," Enolia called to the bookseller at the refreshment table. "And will someone give her a seat, please?"

An older man got up, but the mom waved him off, smiled at Enolia and retreated to the children's section to watch. Alden felt for her. Not everyone wanted to be in the spotlight, and Enolia seemed to be going out of her way to embarrass people. Maybe she'd been a standup comic in a previous life.

He looked at Roz, who shrugged. But she also had a question in her hazel eyes. What did Roz know that he didn't?

"Now, where was I?" Enolia asked the crowd.

"You were going to tell us a story!" a man called from the third row.

"That's right. I was," she said. "But you know what I'd rather do right now? Read you a scene from my book. Would you like that?"

Cheers greeted her proposal. She could've proposed baking more book cookies and gotten the same reaction, Alden suspected. But he was excited to hear her read, too. Theatrics aside, her books always kept him hooked.

Enolia moved behind the podium, donned a pair of reading glasses that had been stowed there, and opened the book to a spot denoted by a big, obvious bookmark. She ran her finger down the page. "Now just let me find it ..."

She lifted her eyes to the audience before she looked down and read, "The body of Renda Child retained a ghastly beauty that reminded Detective Harbaugh of the last time he'd seen her, pale and far too thin, as she stalked the runway in New York."

Enolia surveyed the crowd, enjoying her fans' murmurs, then their rapt hush ... until a piercing scream shattered the silence.

ROZ'S HEAD whipped toward the sound as half the audience stood and even Enolia startled. Not part of her act, then, she thought.

"Who was that?" Roz asked as everyone started talking at once.

"*Where* was that?" Alden exclaimed. "Out back, I think." And he was off and running, pausing only long enough to down the rest of the champagne and plop down the glass.

Roz wasn't going to let him have all the fun. She sprinted behind him as he skirted Enolia and plunged into the back hallway. A couple of other men were on their heels, ready to help whoever was in crisis.

She practically ran into Alden's back after he burst through the back door of the bookstore. He'd stopped just outside, then took a hesitant step forward. Roz had to step aside to see around him. She sort of wished she hadn't.

A woman crouched next to a figure crumpled on the pavement, a man whose jacket and hair showed signs of burns.

Roz knew him by his shoes. Because not enough was left of his face to identify Wayne Vandershell.

"Are you all right?" Alden was asking.

No, Roz thought, but then she realized Alden was talking to the hysterical woman. It was Sheryl.

Oh, no.

This was horrible.

And it was going to be extra complicated to cover this story if their correspondent was involved. Roz hated herself for thinking of that right now, but it was a fact, and they had to deal with it. This was a story, and given it happened at a reading by the famous Enolia Honeywood, it was potentially a big one.

Sheryl looked up at Alden. "It's Wayne," she gasped.

"Come away from—come away from him," Roz said. She'd almost said "Come away from the body." She was ninety-nine percent sure it was a body, but Sheryl didn't need to hear that word right now.

Roz stepped forward and helped Alden guide Sheryl away from the former Mr. Vandershell.

"You," Roz snapped at one of the horrified men gaping at the scene. "Call 9-1-1. Ask for police and an ambulance."

Just in case, she thought. But she knew in her heart they were going to need the medical examiner.

Roz heard the man's call as she wrapped her arms around the trembling Sheryl, who sobbed into her shoulder. People spoke behind her, disembodied voices. Alden told curiosity-seekers who'd come to the back door to stay inside. Mae exclaimed and then ushered everyone in. Enolia, apparently speaking from the hallway, offered to continue the reading, but Mae asked her to move on to the book signing.

Which all felt sort of weird, but it would be even weirder to hear Enolia Honeywood perform a scene about a murder when it looked like one had just occurred in the alley behind the shop.

Two strips of businesses on parallel streets backed up to this alley. It was a through road, but it was barely big enough for a trash truck, and it was one-way. It didn't get much traffic. Still, a killer could've driven or even walked through here with no trouble at all, if that was what happened.

Was there a killer? Or was this an accident?

All of this went through Roz's brain as she patted Sheryl's back and forced herself to look over the woman's shoulder at the scene. At the body. It was a mess.

Alden quietly took notes on his phone and, even more quietly, a couple of photos. They would never run anything that graphic in *The Courier-Beacon*, but photos were information, and they were going to need as much information as they could get.

Just then, Hai slipped out the back door, camera in hand. Roz knew he'd try to get something tasteful they could run in the paper. But she didn't want to be in a photo, and she didn't want Sheryl in one, either. She shook her head slightly at him and pointed to the scene, and he nodded and changed angles.

Sirens sounded, closing quickly. That was one good thing about a small town—the police were never far away. The guy who'd made the phone call was hanging back, trying not to look. The other one had gone inside the back door, mumbling something about keeping people away. Which was a good idea, because this had crime scene written all over it.

Her eyes strayed back to the body, then drifted to something in the street. Pieces of something? Was that some kind of shotgun shell? She didn't know much about guns, but Alden did. She'd ask him later.

The sirens were loud, now, and Roz blinked as new players

entered the scene. She released Sheryl to a female medic from the newly arrived ambulance. The other paramedic knelt to examine Wayne Vandershell. It took him only a moment to verify what Roz already suspected.

It wasn't him who said what she was thinking, though.

"This doesn't look good," came a familiar voice behind her. She turned around. It was Deputy Duke Dawson, an old friend and occasional date back in high school, with thick golden-brown hair and a perpetual sunburn. He was accompanied by brown-skinned Officer Naya Byrd, her black hair pinned in a neat bun, her sharp, dark eyes taking an inventory of the details.

"Is he dead?" Duke asked.

"Yes," Roz and the paramedic said at the same time.

"Sorry," Roz added. "I'm a little shook up."

"Roz." Duke gave her a look of kind concern. "Did you find him?"

"No, Sheryl did. Sheryl Pugh." Roz pointed to Sheryl, who now leaned against the bumper in the open back doors of the ambulance with a blanket around her shoulders, talking to the paramedic.

"We came out of the bookstore when we heard her scream," Alden added.

Duke's eyes narrowed. He'd made it clear he didn't like Alden much, partly because Duke hadn't quite given up an interest in Roz. "Did you touch anything?"

"No, sir," Alden said.

"Me neither," Roz added.

Duke sighed. "Good. Naya, I'll call the ME if you call FIS." The medical examiner and the forensic team, Roz realized.

"No problem. And you two need to step back," Officer Byrd told the reporters. "Way back. Into the store."

"We're not doing any harm here," Roz said.

"Now, Roz, you have to let us do our job," Duke said. "You've seen all you can see anyway. We can talk later." He lifted an eyebrow, and she got it. He'd give her more than he put in the police report, but she had to play nice.

"Fine. Let me say a word to Sheryl before we go." She walked over to the ambulance, not asking permission first. Because she knew Sheryl would be Duke's next stop after his phone call.

"Sheryl, are you OK?" Roz asked her.

Sheryl let out a shuddering sigh. The medic patted her shoulder and walked toward the body, leaving them alone. "I'll be OK, I guess. It's just such a shock."

"I know. I'm sorry. Listen, the police are going to want to talk to you. I advise you to get a lawyer. If you don't have one, give me a call. I'll see if our publisher can lend you ours."

"But this has nothing to do with the paper," Sheryl said.

"Maybe not, but you might be treated as a suspect." Roz lowered her voice, spotting Duke walking toward them as Alden hovered by the back door. "Do you have a lawyer?"

"If there's one thing I got out of my divorce, it's a lawyer. I'll call her right now and see what she says. I think she has a colleague who can help me."

"Good." Roz gave her a hug.

"Thanks for being so nice." Sheryl's reddened face and watery eyes tweaked Roz's heart.

"Of course. I'm so sorry."

"Roz? It's time." Duke had his hands on his duty belt and a small frown on his lips.

"All right. I'll call you later," she told Sheryl, then nodded at Duke and slipped by him before he could say anything else. Officer Byrd was across the alley, on her phone.

Roz met up with Alden by the door and tried not to look at the body, but the image was burned in her brain. She felt a little shaky.

Alden slipped an arm around her and guided her into the back hallway of the shop, past the two restrooms, a closet and the office.

"Did you tell Sheryl to get a lawyer?" he murmured.

"Of course."

"Good girl."

Roz lifted an eyebrow at him. "Duke won't think so."

"Maybe Duke likes bad girls."

"But I'm always good."

"Except when you're not," Alden purred.

She snorted softly, feeling her face heat. Maybe it was an inappropriate time to flirt, but his teasing took her mind off what they'd just seen. And knowing Alden, that was exactly what he'd intended.

They reentered the main room. Enolia Honeywood sat at the table by the podium, signing books. It appeared she'd already worked through most of the queue; maybe a dozen people remained.

"Did you get a book?" Roz asked Alden.

"No, I didn't. I guess I won't now."

"You should."

Alden gave her a funny look. "Really?"

"Yes. I want Enolia to know your face. And I want you to tell her you write for the paper and want an interview."

Alden smiled. "So we can ask her about what happened here today."

"Not just that, but yeah. You can get your celebrity gossip, too."

"With a side of murder," he said. "I'll do it."

chapter
four

"I CAN'T BELIEVE she said yes so fast," Alden said as he guided his Miata toward the beach. He relished the drive down palm-tree-lined streets, even if he didn't put the top down. He wanted Roz to be happy, and Roz said she didn't want to show up at Enolia's house with convertible hair.

"I can't believe I'm spending my Saturday afternoon off working," Roz replied.

"You know you couldn't resist this story. And at least we got to have a nice lunch at the E-Tea Room."

"Weird lunch," said Roz. "Everyone was so freaked out."

"Violent death does that to people. I hoped we might get some good gossip in there, given it filled up with Enolia Honeywood fans right after the signing. But mostly they just chattered about what we already know."

"Which isn't much," Roz pointed out. "You got good quotes, though." She shot him a warm look that made him want to skip the interview and take her somewhere with a bed. A big, bouncy bed.

But they were already neck-deep in this story. They'd spent an hour and a half at the *Beacon* office—er, *The Courier-Beacon,* he reminded himself—putting together a quick article for the website, including a couple of Hai's photos. Everyone else was off today—one of the joys of working for a small-town, weekly newspaper. When news broke on the weekend, Roz almost always stepped up. Given this story was right up Alden's alley, he had to join her. Besides, he wanted to. Working with her was pure fun.

They'd tried to dig up background information on Wayne Vandershell, but there wasn't a lot. Google led them to one of those sites full of entertainment profiles and credits, where he was listed as producer on a few films Alden had never heard of. He had a couple of social media accounts that mostly showed him hobnobbing at film festivals. And his name didn't come up on any county property or criminal records. Sheryl had told Roz that Wayne was "putting down roots here," but if that was the case, they couldn't see the trees or the forest.

"Why do you think Enolia was so amenable to talking to you today?" Roz asked.

"Convenience, I suppose. Maybe she wants to get her press out of the way. She has a book to push."

"I suppose she needs to do publicity like everyone else, but it's already on the bestseller lists."

"Fear not. Soon, all your questions will be answered," he intoned with mock gravity.

"If only. Speaking of ... that *was* a murder scene back there, wasn't it? I thought maybe he'd been shot," Roz said. "Did you see that debris on the ground? Was there a shell casing?"

Alden winced at the thought of Wayne lying there. "I'll have to look at the phone photos. I confess, I didn't dwell on the scene. I didn't want to look at it any longer than necessary. It was ugly. I guess we have to ask why someone would shoot him. A robbery?"

"Maybe not. I texted Duke earlier to ask if Wayne had been robbed, and he told me he still had a wallet full of cash in his pocket."

"You texted Duke?" Alden tried not to sound jealous. "And why wasn't that in our story?"

"He asked me to hold that information back for now, in case it's relevant to the death. I agreed because I expect more from him later. I don't want to burn him."

"Seems to me Deputy Duke gets a lot of latitude."

"He's helpful. You know that." Roz wore a mischievous little smile. "And I think he secretly likes being a source."

"Mm-hmm." Alden turned north on the road closest to the beach, lined with beach emporiums and hotels—a mix of kitschy mid-century properties and more recent high-rises, resorts and swank boutique establishments.

Comet Cove was named for the two famous comets that buzzed Earth in 1910. The community was sleepy for a long time, as the old-timers tell it, though the inlet made it attractive to fishing and pleasure boats. During the moon-shot days of the 1960s, whose epicenter was a few towns north in Cape Canaveral, there was a population boom. The town leaned in to its spacey identity. More hotels sprouted, too.

Just in the past decade, celebrities began to discover the scenic town, carving out a haven for themselves. Their wealthy publisher joined the invasion and started *The Beacon* to compete with the *Comet Cove Courier*, luring Alden from his tabloid job earlier this year to pursue the glitterati.

The biggest testament to the influx of stars was in the houses along the beach. The character of the road changed as they drove north into more exclusive residential neighborhoods. The few remaining bungalows and groovy wooden surf shacks were being leveled in favor of ritzy stucco palaces with gated driveways.

Enolia Honeywood's house was one of these. A tall hedge flanked the gate. Beyond the black vertical bars, a wall covered with a vine dripping with hot-pink bougainvillea flowers hid the house.

Alden pulled up to the gate and pressed a button on the intercom mounted on a post next to the driveway.

A minute later, a man's voice replied. "Yes?"

"Alden Knox and Roz Melander from *The Courier-Beacon* to see Ms. Honeywood," Alden said.

"She's expecting you." A buzz sounded, and the gate slowly slid aside.

"Kai didn't seem all that upset that Enolia didn't want us to bring a photographer," Roz noted as Alden drove them in.

"Can you blame him? She seemed to enjoy putting him on the spot." Alden navigated around the wall, which turned out to be part of a detached three-car garage. He pulled up in front of a huge, modern two-story house the soft pink of strawberry ice cream. "Besides, I can always take a few photos with my phone."

"If she'll let you."

"She'll let me." Alden grinned and turned off the car, and they got out.

"Planning on trading up, are you?" Roz teased him as they headed to the grand front door. It faced a generous lawn with islands of lush tropical landscaping, enclosed by the hedge along the road.

"Never." He leaned in and kissed her neck, reveled in her sigh, and pressed the doorbell.

It rang with a profound *ding-dong*. The door opened to

reveal Craig, Enolia's nerdy assistant from the signing. Why was he here?

To wrangle us, Alden thought.

"Have you sufficiently recovered?" Alden asked Craig, still in his bow tie, the brown fringe around his bald pate neatly trimmed.

A wrinkle briefly formed in Craig's brow. "Recovered from the signing? That was a perfect crowd."

"But a not so perfect situation."

Craig adjusted his spectacles. "The important thing is to move forward and present a happy front. Enolia is the happy front. *She* is the reader experience."

I thought books were the reader experience, Alden thought as he and Roz followed Craig through an airy foyer that opened into a two-story living area. Two columns painted with large green leaves and flowering vines supported the high ceiling. A wall of windows and sliding glass doors looked out on a swimming pool and, beyond it, palm trees and the sparkling blue ocean.

Fat, cushy white furniture lay about on a sand-colored travertine floor, interspersed with three modern floor lamps—white shades mounted atop wooden tripods of different sizes. A round wooden coffee table sat on a kaleidoscopic rug in front of the couch.

A white custom shelf unit took up most of one wall. At its center was a closed cabinet painted with colorful flowers—hiding a TV, maybe? Below it, an electric fireplace blazed with imposter flames, throwing no heat. The staggered shelves' contents alternated between showy pieces of strategically lit glass art, a few personal photos, and books, most of them Enolia's. Her art tastes ran to bold paintings of flowers, much like the TV cabinet. Colorful but surprisingly boring.

"Have a seat. I'll be back in a moment." Craig moved off

toward a showroom kitchen that was partially visible through a wide doorway.

"If I sit on that couch, I'll fall asleep." Roz eyed it hungrily just the same.

"It does look cozy." Alden raised a flirty eyebrow, and Roz shot him one of her *Can't you be responsible for five minutes?* looks. He laughed.

She plopped down at one end of it anyway and beckoned him over. "I want to sit next to you, not Craig," she whispered as he settled in beside her and pulled out his phone, revving up the recording app.

Craig returned with a tray holding a pitcher filled with pale yellow liquid and lemon slices, tall glasses, an ice bucket and a plate of Enolia book cookies. He set the tray on the coffee table and sat next to Alden.

"Is that real lemonade?" Roz asked with interest as Craig used a silver scoop to fill the glasses with ice.

"Yes, I made it myself." Craig smiled. "Would you like some?"

"Yes, please," she said, and Alden also took a glass.

"I hope you don't mind the cookies," Craig said. "We had a few left over."

"Did you make those, too?" Alden asked.

"No," he said. "They're from Cosmic Confections."

"Craig has many skills," came Enolia's strong alto voice, "but baking isn't one of them." The writer strode into the room, now wearing relaxed tan linen pants, matching sandals and a loose white blouse. Her white-blond hair hung straight. If she stood still, she would've been camouflaged by her own furniture, given away only by her pink lipstick. "Welcome to my home."

"It's beautiful," said Roz, rising with Alden to greet their hostess. "You have a wonderful view."

"Thank you. I find beachside living agrees with me."

"You were in Upstate New York before?" Alden confirmed.

Enolia smiled, acknowledging that he did his homework. "Yes. I still have a home there for when the summer heat here gets too unbearable."

Of course she does. "It's a pretty part of the country."

"You know it?" she asked.

He just nodded, not wanting to get into his contentious relationship with his family there. "Thanks for giving us time this afternoon. Should we talk in here?"

"Perfect." She sat in a large chair next to a small table stacked with a few books. "Craig, I'll take a lemonade. I've already pre-gamed with Tums."

Alden and Roz both laughed and sat.

Alden got Enolia's permission to record, then embarked on several questions about her books and writing, hinted that he'd love to see her office—"maybe later," she said—and warmed her up with his unabashed love of her work. It was a thrill to talk to her about her novels, as cynical as he was about celebrities in general. Writing still held magic for him.

"Any romance in your life?" Alden asked. He had to. You could take the reporter out of the tabloid, but it was hard to take the tabloid out of the reporter.

Enolia smirked. "Not at the moment. And I'm not in the market, in spite of what dear Mae said at the signing."

"Oh? So no future Mr. Honeywood in the works, then?"

She looked amused. "Probably never. I assume you know my divorce was final twenty years ago. Best thing I ever did. Don't get me wrong. I'm not pooh-poohing marriage. Everyone should get married at least once."

Alden and Roz both chuckled. Craig just smiled. Maybe he'd heard the joke before.

"Mae said your *Shellbreak Island* is going to be a movie?" Alden asked.

A slight frown touched her lips. "I'm not so sure now, if what I heard about the unpleasantness behind the bookstore today is true."

"What did you hear?" Roz asked, wrapping her napkin around half of the big book cookie she'd nibbled when Alden was on a roll.

Enolia swallowed and took a breath. "That the man who died was someone who was going to make my dream of a film adaptation a reality."

Roz sat up straighter. "You knew Wayne Vandershell?"

"I did. He's—he was a film producer. He committed to producing *Shellbreak Island*." Enolia's eyes unfocused, gazing toward the ocean, as she mused. "He was so charming. I've talked with these movie people before, you know. My agent set up meetings. Nothing ever came from it. But Wayne sought me out. He talked me into a drink. He ran into me after my weekly lunch at Sirenia with my pickleball club—we play at Lunaria Lodge on Wednesdays." Her smile held a hint of sadness. "Maybe he was stalking me a bit, but I didn't mind. I thought him rather clever. I was flattered."

"More lemonade?" Craig interrupted at what Alden considered an inopportune time.

"No, thanks," Alden and Roz said simultaneously, then exchanged a glance.

"Had you signed a contract with Mr. Vandershell?" Roz asked.

Craig interrupted again. "I don't think these are the kinds

of details Ms. Honeywood should be discussing with you," he said pointedly to Alden, not Roz.

Why me? Alden was trying to shed his tabloid reputation and thought he'd been doing a pretty good job. Who was this Craig, anyway?

"It's all right, Craig." Enolia focused again on the reporters. "We had an agreement. Some papers were signed, but you know how the movie business is. It's all options and pitches until someone books the caterer, signs the director and actors, and sticks them in front of the camera."

Interesting, even if she was stingy with details. "What do you know about Wayne?" Alden asked.

"He was great at making connections, which is not one of my skills. I know that may come as a surprise," she said, reading his expression, "but while I'm good on stage, I rarely get close to people. Wayne did." She closed her eyes for a moment. "I'm getting a bit tired, speaking of being on stage. It's been a long day."

Craig stood instantly and turned to Roz and Alden. "I'll show you out."

Alden ignored him and turned his winningest smile on Enolia. "Could I take a quick photo of you first for the newspaper? It would mean so much to get a photo of you here in Comet Cove. Outside of the bookstore, I mean."

She perked up a bit. "All right. Where do you want me?"

"Your office?"

"Not today. How about here?" She pointed to a spot on the bookshelves where a lot of her titles were on display.

"Sure." Alden and Roz stood.

"Let me help you out." Roz pulled a real camera from her big purse, and Alden suppressed a chuckle. He didn't need his phone after all. Roz was a good photographer in her own right, and as always, she came prepared.

She gently directed Enolia and moved around, hitting the shutter fast, getting close-up shots and wider views of the author with her shelves, the fireplace, and the art, taking advantage of the excellent light from the big windows.

Craig had whisked away the refreshments to discourage their lingering while Roz took her photos. She was done in less than ten minutes. Not overstaying their welcome was a good idea, because Alden had a feeling he'd want to talk with Enolia again and didn't want to tick her off.

"Thanks so much for your time. I can't wait to read the book," Alden told her as Craig rematerialized, ready to escort them to the door.

"My pleasure," Enolia said, giving off performer vibes again. Had they gotten the real Enolia at all today?

"Thank you," Roz echoed, and they were out the door and heading to his snappy red car.

He took a moment to pull down the convertible's soft-top roof so they could enjoy the pleasant evening as hints of sunset oranges and purples touched the sky. Roz pulled an elastic tie out of her bag and secured her hair once they got into the car.

Alden drove them up to the gate, which slowly slid aside. "What do you think?"

"I think I want to learn more about Wayne Vandershell. I feel like there's a lot she didn't tell us."

"So do I." Alden turned south on the beach road.

"Let's process what we have and figure out where to go next. And I'll ping Duke, too."

"Oh, goody," Alden said.

Roz laughed. "Want to get some dinner?"

"I saw you palm that half a cookie. That not enough for you?"

"Ha. I figure I'll have it for breakfast. Those things are huge."

"Not quite as thick as Enolia's books, but close." He glanced at her. "Seafood?"

"I see food. I eat it. That's the problem."

Alden gave her an appreciative look. "You're gorgeous."

"Oh, shut up." But she grinned just the same.

"It's a beautiful evening, and I know a good place in Bohemia Beach. Up for a ride?"

She gave him the side-eye at his sultry tone. "Sure. As long as you get me home in time to do some research."

"I might not get you home at all."

She quirked her mouth. "That might also be acceptable."

Yes, he thought. Research could wait until the morning.

chapter
five

"TELL me again why both of you need to work on this story?" John Restyn leaned back in his chair and popped his gum. The *Beacon* editor had stayed on after the merger, apparently content with the small raise that came with the doubling of his tiny staff, which Roz only knew about because she'd been privy to all the financial details. The deal had saved her family paper's legacy and given her ailing mother enough money to retire and move into a senior community in northwest Comet Cove where she could get the care she needed.

"Roz is good at the financial and government angles," Alden told John. "And I'm good at the other things."

"I think you've both proven you're capable of all the things, and this is one dead guy," John said, pushing his glasses up onto his head, where they almost got lost in his chaotic, gray-streaked black hair. They left behind pink marks on either side of his nose. He wore a golf shirt and khakis, standard office fare in Florida.

For this Monday morning meeting, Roz and Alden had cleared off two chairs to sit in front of John's desk. Issues of the colorful *Courier-Beacon*—much more colorful than the

Courier had ever been—were stacked next to empty coffee cups, full pen holders, an Orlando City lion mascot bobble head, and photos of his twin girls.

"And what financial and government angles are you talking about?" John pressed.

"We did a lot of research yesterday, and then we called Sheryl and talked to her again," Roz said. She and Alden had spent most of Sunday at his apartment on their respective computers, trying to track down anything they could about Wayne Vandershell.

John's eyes lit up with interest under his bushy brows, and he looked through his glass wall into the bullpen to see if the freelancer had appeared. She hadn't, though a few other reporters were out there. "Is she a suspect?"

"Not yet," Roz hedged. "But she's got a lawyer."

John nodded. "Good. So what did she tell you?"

"She and Wayne had a casual relationship," Alden said.

Roz gave him a sidelong glance. "I'm not so sure she thought it was casual."

John smirked. "And?"

"And she said again that Wayne was putting down roots here," Roz said. "And that he was creating a movie studio in Comet Cove."

"Remember I told you I'd heard rumors?" Alden added. "I think they were about Wayne Vandershell."

John sat up. "Where? Details?"

This was where Roz knew they had a lot of work to do. "We're still working on that, but Sheryl said he had a partner who was seeking permits. She also said she didn't know who the partner was."

"Sure she doesn't," Alden said.

Roz frowned at him before turning back to John. "I think

she's telling the truth. I want to find out who it was. They could know more about him. And if they were filing for permits, there's a paper trail."

"Could the partner have killed him?" John speculated.

"We're a long way from knowing that," Roz said.

"We don't have motive either," Alden added. "Wayne was apparently the golden boy who made Hollywood dreams come true."

"Wayne Vandershell was going to make Enolia Honeywood's first hit book into a movie," Roz affirmed. "Maybe more. And Sheryl said he was going to produce her screenplay, too."

"Sheryl writes scripts?" John didn't sound convinced.

Roz shrugged. "Her gardening columns don't have any dialogue. Maybe it's her secret weapon."

"Maybe a shotgun is her secret weapon," John said.

"Come on. You don't believe that," Roz answered.

Alden cut in. "We're not even sure if that's what killed him. I don't think that was a shotgun shell on the ground, but it's hard to tell from my photos, and Hai didn't get many shots of the carnage."

"Then what killed the man?" John asked.

"No official word. And Duke hasn't returned my phone calls," Roz admitted.

"Is the honeymoon over?" John snarked.

"Hey," Alden said. "If she's having a honeymoon with anybody, it's me."

Roz's gaze snapped to his.

"I mean ... uh ..." Alden looked sheepish, but the embers burning in his gray eyes were only for her.

Her heart fluttered even as she lifted a scolding eyebrow.

She wanted their relationship to be invisible at work, even though the editor was well aware of what was going on.

She turned back to John. "Duke and Deputy Byrd are heading up the investigation, and they were busy yesterday. And the sheriff wasn't thrilled that Alden and I were on the scene before they were, so Duke is lying low. He'll get back to me today. I'm sure of it."

John sighed. "All right. The wire already picked up the story since it happened at an Enolia Honeywood signing, and I don't want anybody coming in and scooping us in our backyard. I'm sure the city is freaking out over another celebrity-adjacent death, especially after all that fuss a couple of months ago. This is a quiet town, usually, and they want the money to keep rolling in."

"And our publisher does, too," Alden pointed out.

John grimaced. "Which means I can't waste my reporter resources. Get me something that makes it worth my while to have both of you on the story. We need to get something fresh online today, too."

"Will do," Roz said.

"And I want that feature on Enolia Honeywood to run Friday, which means you need to turn it around by Wednesday," John told Alden.

Alden gave him a pleading look. "Not Thursday?"

"Wednesday," John insisted. "I want to run it with a story about the murder. Which means you two need to get cracking. Roz, let me know what the others are doing, OK? I want a budget by noon."

"Sure." She got up, and Alden followed her out of John's office.

Roz was both a reporter and the managing editor, a big title that didn't mean much at a small publication like this one. It was a nod to her role at the erstwhile *Courier*. And it meant they really had her doing multiple jobs for the price of one, including writing and editing and wrangling the junior staff. Which meant she had to come up with a story budget including summaries, story lengths and art possibilities so they could plan Friday's edition. She'd done most of that already, but she had to make sure everyone was on track.

She studied Alden as he sat at his desk, complete with his own piles of paper, a bust of Shakespeare wearing a Bohemia Beach bucket hat, and the hidden book of poetry filled with Donne and Marvell and compatriots that he didn't think anyone knew about. A poet with a cynical shell. Her ... boyfriend? Lover?

Her employee? Ugh. No. But she did have to manage him a little bit, even though she left most of that to John, since the men had worked together before she came along.

Could she manage her feelings?

That was another question entirely.

ALDEN FINISHED CHECKING HIS EMAIL, grabbed his cooling coffee cup and sat at the table in the center of the bullpen, the open area outside the glass offices. He glanced at the biggest fishbowl, where publisher Webb Howard would sit if he ever actually appeared. His executive assistant, Helen, focused on her computer in his outer office, also behind glass, as was John on the perpendicular wall. A rarely used conference room sat next to John's office.

Maybe they were fish in a bowl. But they also had a private space Alden envied and nice views from the second-story windows, with the town laid out before them and glimpses of the ocean several blocks beyond.

"Gather round, folks," Roz called out from the seat she'd claimed at the head of the table. The reporters in the room stopped chatting and scrolling their laptops and dragged themselves over, plunking down beverages and notebooks.

Alden turned his attention to his colleagues. A few had worked with him when *The Beacon* was just *The Beacon*: Kat McClure, stylish and red-haired, whom celebrities genuinely liked but who could write anything with verve and often covered bigger news stories. Tim Shepard, a short fair-skinned guy with shaggy brown hair and a beard who kept locals happy with his coverage of high school sports and the publisher happy with peppy pieces about the pro golfers who came to the recently expanded club near the wildlife refuge, Vesper Lakes.

Then there were the *Courier* refugees: young Bruce Price, pale with bristling dark hair, a native who backed up Tim on sports and covered more hard news, post-merger. Janice Darby, with dancing, dark eyes and light-brown skin, who did a bang-up job covering environmental issues, a new beat for *The Courier-Beacon*. She also wrote about schools and families— though she was single like everyone except Tim. Then again, they were all pretty young, as reporters tended to be at this level and size of publication.

Hai appeared at the top of the open stairs—the floor below housed the ad and production departments. He strolled over and dumped his camera backpack next to a chair before he plopped down. "Sorry I'm late."

Alden was struck by how much he looked like his mother, Mrs. Yung, who ran the Meteor Mart. Same spiky black hair and angled cheekbones. Only Hai was several inches taller.

"Hi, Hai," all the reporters said with the usual teasing tone.

The shooter gave them a withering look. "Never gets old."

The corner of Roz's mouth turned up as she scanned them. "Let's do this quickly, all right? Alden and I have to get on this story."

"Get it on, you mean," Bruce mumbled to giggles.

Roz's hazel eyes lasered in on his. "Bruce, did I just hear you volunteer to cover the zoning board meeting this afternoon?"

"No, I—"

"Great, I'll put you down for that. Talk to Janice about the impact of that new southside subdivision near the river so you ask good questions. And let me know if they talk about a movie studio, OK?"

"OK," Bruce mumbled into his chest as the others snickered.

"Janice, what's happening with the wildlife preserve?"

"Construction has started on the parking lot, the nature center, and a boardwalk trail over the wetland. They're planning to create a couple of paths, though they're keeping most of it wild," Janice said. "The nudists aren't happy, though."

"The nudists?" Alden asked.

"There's a small beach on the south end that's been popular with a local nudist group for years," Roz said. "Officials overlooked it because they didn't see the harm."

"But now most of the council thinks it doesn't fit the 'family-friendly' vibe they want," Janice added. "The nudists are planning a protest tomorrow morning."

"You'd better go to that," Roz said. "You too, Hai. But keep it PG."

"I'll try to find some palm fronds I can shoot through." Hai's remark prompted more chuckles.

Round Roz went, getting story statuses, making sure art was assigned, asking questions. Alden loved watching her work. She didn't just break their balls. She complimented them on their good work, too. "Great photos Saturday, Hai. Tasteful. And we'll use the book signing pics with Alden's story about Enolia Honeywood."

"I saw yours in the system, too," he said. "Nice."

She smiled. "I just took advantage of our access. But thanks. OK, everybody—email me your updated budget lines."

And they were off.

Alden stood and sidled over to her. "You're so good."

"Don't think you're getting special treatment," she quipped, soft enough so only he could hear.

"I expect *very* special treatment."

Her face turned pink, and he bit back a smile.

"Don't make me send you to the zoning meeting," she said.

"That might not be a bad idea. Especially if they talk about the movie studio."

"That's what I want to nail down, whether such a thing even exists. Sheryl was scant on details." She moved to her desk at the edge of the room—she'd been offered the glassed-in conference room as an office after the merger but turned it down—and he sat in the chair next to it, facing her.

"I'm going to work one of my sources at City Hall, see what they can tell me," she continued. "Have you been able to learn any more about Wayne Vandershell's movies?"

He shook his head. "I can dig some more while you make your calls. Then we can confer?"

"Deal." She quirked her mouth at him. "Then we can 'get it on.'"

Alden snorted. "I haven't hazed that boy properly. Give me time."

Roz smiled. "Whipper-snappers."

"Says the old lady of thirty-two," he threw over his shoulder as he returned to his desk. He was only a couple of years older than she was, but after all he'd seen, sometimes it felt like decades.

He opened his computer to dig. On Sunday, they'd found a few facts about Wayne's undistinguished youth in California and a couple of references to him attending UCLA film school. There was almost nothing online about what he'd been doing since then. And there was only so much information web surfing could unearth, especially when it came to the entertainment business. Celebrity-chasers reported rumors as fact. Even if a movie deal was real, so many films never came to fruition. It was hard to know what stories to trust. *Oh, the irony.* He'd fed that rumor mill himself.

He went back and checked the film database site they'd looked at yesterday and Wayne Vandershell's credits. He had a short film picked for a few festivals, though it apparently hadn't made it online yet. A student film, maybe? It was more than ten years old. Shouldn't it be on YouTube by now? And there were other producer credits, but as creative as Alden got in his searches, he couldn't find more information on the movies. A couple of them had release dates in the past. Had they gone straight to video? Maybe with a new name? It happened.

Vandershell had a few older credits as crew, too. One was on a heist movie he'd actually heard of, *Fastest Spin Wins*. Alden recognized another name in the credits, an assistant director he'd written nice things about—a guy Alden had had a few beers with in LA who was now frying much larger fish.

As Alden opened his contacts on his phone, he startled as a hand lightly touched his shoulder.

It was Roz. "Am I interrupting something?"

He spun to face her. "I was focused, is all. Tracking something down."

"Good. I've got a lead. But I want to talk to my mom about it."

He looked up at her in surprise. "OK. Want to ping me afterward? I might have more on Vandershell by then."

"Sounds good. We can grab a quick lunch and see where to go from there, OK?"

He grinned. "Get it on, Ms. Melander. Get it on."

ROZ DROVE her silver hybrid across Comet Cove to the northwest quarter of town, well north of Star Inlet. Her mother's building overlooked a small bay in the Indian River Lagoon. Or the river, as locals called it.

Clouds scudded across the sky, spattering raindrops on the windshield, but after Roz parked she skipped digging out an umbrella. She clutched her big leather bag tightly to her chest and trotted across the nicely landscaped parking lot to the multi-winged, eight-story pile of concrete known as Daydream Village.

More of a compound than a village, it was considered a skyscraper around these parts, but the city council reluctantly approved it knowing there was a need for retiree communities, especially one like this. If Megan Melander's multiple sclerosis became too advanced for her to live independently in her apartment, she'd have options for higher levels of care.

Roz walked through the spacious lobby with its coffee shop, lovely decor and bright open spaces where people sat reading newspapers (*yes!*), playing mah jongg, assembling puzzles and having small, cheerful meetings. This place offered all kinds of hobby spaces and activities, a cafeteria if folks didn't want to cook, and visiting helpers for hire. Her mom had a woman come in a couple of days a week.

Roz moved past a bank of mailboxes to the head of one wing and hit the button for the elevator.

This was nice, wasn't it? Roz had mixed feelings about her mom's move here after Megan sold the *Courier* to the *Beacon*'s publisher. As a dutiful daughter, Roz couldn't shake a primal guilt about not stepping up to be a caretaker. But this was absolutely what Megan wanted. She wanted Roz to carry on the legacy of the *Courier*, the newspaper Roz's grandparents founded that Megan and David, Roz's dad, made a pillar of the community.

David died close to two years ago of a heart attack. With her mother ailing and the paper struggling, Roz gave up her rising Baltimore journalism career to come back and run it. Then Alden and the big story and the merger happened, and her mom could afford to move.

The elevator opened onto a clean, quiet, carpeted corridor of apartments on the fifth floor. Doors were set back in small alcoves that residents decorated as if they were front porches in a suburban neighborhood: bouquets of fake flowers, seasonal tchotchkes, ceramic dogs and cats, even small bits of framed art. Precious bits people couldn't get rid of even if they knew they no longer had room for them. Life overflow, Roz thought. You built up your life and then you shrunk it down again.

She found Megan's door, which had a faux topiary bush next to it, a matching square wreath around the peephole, and a framed picture on the short adjoining wall that had been different every time she visited. This time it was a black-and-white photo of what this very site looked like before

Daydream Village—a ramshackle fish camp with weathered wooden boats. Roz felt a twinge. Old Florida was endangered if not completely gone. But her mom had a nice place to live.

The door opened a few moments after her knock, and Megan waved her in and enveloped her in a hug. "Roz! I didn't expect you today."

"Spontaneous visit. Am I interrupting anything?"

"Not at all. I have a book club meeting later." Her mom looked well in jeans and a casual light blue top, her gray-streaked reddish hair recently cropped, her green eyes bright. At sixty-eight, she was practically a kid in this community, though her progressive illness slowed her down. "Want a snack?"

"No, I'm having lunch with Alden later."

"Oh, *Alden*." Megan smiled. "Lucky you. Have a seat then. I'm having a ginger ale with Major Tom."

"Oh, is he drinking soda now? That actually sounds pretty good. I'll grab one, too." Roz took a detour into the small open kitchen, popped a can of ginger ale and poured it over ice in a tall glass. She followed her mom into a roomy living area. It was full of the beachy furniture that came from the old house. A lot of the art had migrated, too, including the black-and-white photos of people and places of Comet Cove, many of which had once run in the newspaper.

Roz set down her bag and sat on the couch next to Major Tom, a beautiful gray cat with golden eyes. He gave her a dour look before lazily rolling onto his back. Roz chuckled and took the invitation to rub his soft belly. "He's not missing many meals, is he?"

"He eats more than I do." Megan sat in her favorite armchair, and they both looked out of the fifth-floor window toward the river, beautiful even under the gloomy clouds. A misty wall of white descended to the steel-gray water under a brooding mountain of vapor, looking soft and light from up here but, Roz knew from experience, drenching anyone under it with a pounding barrage of rain.

"You like it here?" Roz blurted. Yep, still feeling guilty.

"I love it. No maintenance to worry about. And I feel really good right now. I'm on a new medication. But let's not talk about that." Megan sipped her ginger ale and looked at Roz. "How do you like the house?"

"The house" was in fact the house Roz grew up in. She'd given up her furnished rental bungalow and come to terms with her mom to buy the family's modest 1960s rancher in southwest Comet Cove. She'd kept a few of the things Megan didn't want but had installed some of her own and still had a lot of work to do.

"Honestly, it feels a little weird, but I'm doing some painting and updating. I'm leaning in to the mid-century feel of the kitchen, though."

"That's all hip again," Megan agreed. "And lord knows the house needed some TLC. I'm glad. When is Alden moving in?"

Roz almost choked on her ginger ale. "*Wha-what?*" she sputtered. "We haven't talked about anything like that."

"I like him. I'd jump on that if I were you." Megan waggled her eyebrows.

Roz's face heated. She was jumping on that on the regular, which was a nice change for sure. But she wasn't in a hurry to combine households. "It's awkward enough at work already. Speaking of which, we're working on a story—the death of that man at the book signing Saturday?"

"I read what you have so far. Not a lot, is it?"

Roz grimaced. "That's the problem. We have a lot of irons but no fire. I wanted to ask you something."

Megan looked delighted. "How can I help?"

"We've heard that Wayne Vandershell might've been building a movie studio by the airport and that he might have a partner. So I talked to a source at city hall who said they'd received construction permit applications from a company who owns some warehouses down by the airport. Production facilities were mentioned, and some have been approved. The problem is, I can't figure out who really owns the property. It's one of those companies owned by a company that's owned by a company ..."

"And you don't know who it is."

"Right." Roz sighed. "Any idea who that might be?"

"My best guess would be the Esquivels. When the airfield expanded, the airport authority had to buy land from them. If the warehouses are near the airport, that would be a place to start."

"Is there anything they don't own in this county?"

Megan smiled. "Quite a few things, but the family's been here a long time, and they had a lot of property south of the inlet. Some of it was left wild, like the refuge they donated to the town, but they also farmed pineapples and grapefruit back in the day. That's all gone now, of course."

In favor of houses and strip malls, Roz thought. "I met Nicole Esquivel on Saturday. She was at the signing with her kids. Her husband's a developer—Sebastian."

Her mom nodded. "Yes, I've heard of him. One of Antonia's sons, I think. She's the matriarch. But I don't know much about him."

"Maybe the best way to reach him is through Nicole. I'll work that angle and see if they know anything about the warehouses or the project."

"Or the partner," Megan said. "Even if Sebastian Esquivel

says it's not their project, he might know whose project it is. Kind of a long shot, though."

"We have to start somewhere. And Duke isn't calling me back."

"He's jealous," she teased. "But he's a good guy. You'd better get going. You don't want to be late for lunch with Alden."

"Ha! And I have to get some solid reporting in so we can post an update." As she stood and grabbed her bag, Major Tom rolled over and sat up with a grouchy *mrrrow*. "Oh, cat, you have it so good. I don't want to hear it."

Megan laughed. "He sure does."

"Need anything before I go?"

"No. Get out of here." Her mom didn't get up, but she looked good. Content. At least for now. *And now is really all we have, isn't it?*

Roz set her glass in the sink, left the apartment, and texted Duke again as she headed for the elevator.

"DON'T TELL me you've heard about the deal already," Porter Cobb said when he answered the phone, not even giving Alden a chance to say hello.

What deal? Alden, driving and using an earpiece that made Porter's deep voice more gravelly than usual, had a split second to decide whether to play out the string. He settled on greetings first. "Hey, Porter. I guess it's going well then?"

"Getting to direct my dream project in Paris? Hell, yes, it's going well."

"That screenplay you've been fiddling with for years? Fantastic."

"Wait a second." Porter paused. "That's not why you're calling, is it?"

"No, it isn't, but I'm happy for you. I take it this hasn't been announced yet?"

"It hasn't. But I suppose I can't stop you."

Alden chuckled. "Listen, when you're ready, I'll be glad to write something. Especially if it somehow connects with Comet Cove, where I now hang my dashing fedora with the cute little press badge."

Porter snorted. "As if you'd be caught dead in a fedora. You're in Comet Cove? Who're you stalking?"

"You do know I'm out of the tabloids and into local journalism now, right? And I'm stalking whichever celebrity happens to cross my path."

"Alden Knox, reputable journalist. I don't believe it," Porter teased him. "I haven't made it to Comet Cove yet, though I keep hearing people talking about it. I'll look you up when I do."

"You'd better. And I confess, this isn't a purely social call."

"Ah, here it comes. Get out of the road, picklehead!" Porter called out, obviously driving too. "Sorry, tourist was selfie-ing at the Chinese Theatre in the middle of the street. You were saying?"

"I was about to ask you whether you remember a guy named Wayne Vandershell. He worked on the crew for *Fastest Spin Wins*."

"Ooooh, that was a crazy shoot. Let me think." A pause. A honk of a horn. "Refresh my memory."

"I don't know what he looked like then, but he had brown longish hair when I saw him. A pretty good-looking guy, I guess. Supposedly he worked as a video assist operator. I'm not sure what that is."

"A VAO? They show the camera images on video monitors so we, I mean the director mostly but also the crew, can see what's being shot. It can get pretty technical if they integrate simulated visual effects so we can evaluate those kinds of shots on the go, though *Fastest Spin Wins* was mostly live action. Wild car chases."

"And you don't remember Wayne Vandershell?" Alden pushed.

"Maybe I do," Porter mused. "This off the record?"

"It can be."

"Make it so. I don't want to be in the news for anything right now except my movie."

"OK. I don't have to attribute it to you," Alden conceded. "We just want to know more about the guy."

"Fine," Porter said. "He was OK at the job, but I seem to remember him sucking up to anyone who would listen, trying to get them to back his movie."

"What was the pitch?"

"I dunno, some tripe about a struggling writer. Autobiographical. You know the type."

Like me, Alden thought wryly. "And he had no luck?"

"Not then and not ever, I don't think, because I never heard of it getting made. In fact, one day over breakfast bagels, the director told him straight up, 'I could blow smoke up your skirt and tell you I'd do it. Ask you to put up the money to do it. Give you the total runaround. You know why? You smell desperate, and desperate people will do anything. Even your script is about somebody who's desperate for approval and attention and success. And if you're not careful, someone else is going to take advantage of you. I'm just going to do you a favor and say no.'"

"Brutal. Seems like you remember him pretty well, then."

"That's about it."

Alden rattled off the names of the movies Wayne Vandershell listed in his credits, but Porter didn't recognize any of them. "Why do you want to know about him anyway?" his friend asked.

"He got killed on Saturday," Alden replied. "We're trying to figure out why."

"Geez." Porter paused. "That really sucks. Way to bring me down, Knox."

"Sorry. But I appreciate you. Holler if you think of anything else. And keep me updated."

"Will do. I might just come to Comet Cove if you're buying the beer."

"I'll buy the beer *and* write a friendly feature."

"Sounds like a plan. Later."

They clicked off just as Alden pulled into the parking lot that served Comet Cove's small boardwalk. The promenade ran along the northeast side of the inlet to a park and pier facing the ocean.

He flashed back to a memorable ice cream with Roz at the Milky Way, just two doors down from where they were meeting for lunch. They needed to go back there. That was a very good day.

He headed out to the boardwalk. The clouds were starting to clear, and a beam of sunlight hit the causeway bridge to the west, glinting off the cars crossing over it. He admired the boats navigating the inlet and the red-and-white-striped lighthouse across the wide swath of water, a beacon for all.

The Beacon—*The Courier-Beacon*—was aptly named, he thought, as he walked into the diner to meet Roz. Together, maybe they could shed some light on this strange, dark death.

chapter
seven

ROZ HAD NOT TIMED her exit from her mother's building well, and even with the help of the beach towel she kept in her car, she knew she looked like a drenched dog when she walked into the busy Doppler Diner. Her black pants were lightweight and drying, but her sage shirt still felt heavy and damp.

Alden's face lit up when he saw her. He stood until she sat in the booth, which had a nice view of the inlet through the big windows. She didn't know if his smile meant he was laughing or really happy to see her. Or both, which would be fine. And he did look fine in his dark jeans and collared short-sleeved gray shirt. The man had very nice arms.

"You could've gone the extra step and just put on your bathing suit," he said.

Laughing at her then. Or maybe with her. "Ha ha. I got caught in the rain."

"Either that or keel-hauled through the inlet. I like you like this. Very mermaid."

Her long, reddish-brown hair was wavier when wet but also frizzier. Whatever. She'd deal with it later.

After a brief perusal of the menu, they ordered their go-tos

—a hamburger for him, a Reuben for her. This place was classic diner all the way, from the chrome-heavy decor to the counter with barstools to the menu to the vintage jukebox. She loved the vibe. But the food probably wasn't great for her cholesterol.

"Maybe we should try something healthier. Like that Virgo Veggieverse place in town," she suggested as he sipped his coffee and she her iced tea.

Alden raised an eyebrow. "Don't you think they're trying a little too hard with the name?"

"I've seen the menu. It's definitely a veggie-verse."

"No meat at all?"

"Fake meat."

"Ew." He made a face that made her laugh. "And virginal, apparently."

"Virgo, not virginal. Alluding to the constellation, maybe? But I get your point."

"It's pure. Unlike that beautiful burger I'm about to eat. So did Duke get back to you?"

"Oh, crap." She dug into her slightly damp bag and pulled out her phone. "Nope." She shot off another message. He wasn't ignoring her, was he? She put the phone on the table so she could keep an eye on it. "I talked to my mom, though." She explained about the permits for construction of a movie studio at a warehouse complex by the airport and her mom's sugges- tion the Esquivels might own the land.

"So one of them could be Wayne's partner in building the movie studio?"

"That's what I'm hoping to find out this afternoon. Do you have anything?"

"Only that Wayne Vandershell started out as a sad

unwanted screenwriter and tech-crew guy who somehow became a movie producer."

She cocked her head. "Well, that's good color, anyway. Good human interest."

"Maybe, but what puzzles me is how he turned his life around. I talked to a friend in the biz. Said he'd never heard of Vandershell's movies either."

"Is that weird?"

"Maybe not if they were small and they were retitled or something when they got picked up."

They both looked up as their server, a young woman in stretchy black pants and a pink blouse and fifties-style scarf, dropped off plates full of mains and fries. "Anything else?" she asked.

"This looks fabulous," Roz declared, and the server headed off.

Alden didn't hesitate. He took a giant bite of his burger, and a bit of juice dribbled onto his chin. He wiped it away with a napkin before she thought too much about licking it off.

She picked up half of her sandwich and had a bite. *Sooo good* — savory warm corned beef and Swiss all melty together on rye, tangy with sauerkraut and Russian dressing. "So where does this leave us? We need to produce some kind of story today."

"I think we need a comment from the police, even if it's no comment, so we can get a story up," Alden said. "But looking toward print, maybe we can get more from Enolia Honeywood about her connection to the man."

"I just want to know more about her in general. She's mastered the skill of appearing to be open and forthright while being completely cagey."

"I had the same thought," he said. "I wanted to see her office so badly."

"Do you think she's hiding secrets in there?"

"I doubt it, but maybe it reflects more of her interior life. No way it's as boring as her living room is."

Roz chuckled and finished off a fry. "I thought it was very tasteful."

Alden made a theatrical snoring sound and dipped a fry in ketchup before scarfing it down. "Mmm. What do they fry these in?"

"Crack?" Roz ate another one. "I think you should call Enolia back. She has to know something about Wayne's business dealings if he was going to make her book into a film."

"Are the photos you took of her on your laptop? I never got to see them."

"Sure. Hang on a sec." She took another bite of the delicious Reuben. Then she set it down, wiped her hands on a napkin and dug into her bag again. This time she pulled out the computer.

"How much stuff is in that bag?" Alden sipped his coffee.

"Laptop, camera, personal items, a puppy, a small bicycle," she said, cranking up the laptop on the table. In a moment, she'd pulled up the gallery of photos from their interview Saturday afternoon and angled the screen so he could take a look.

"When did you have time to work on these?"

"After I left your place yesterday."

He smiled. "You could've stayed over again."

"I have to sleep sometime."

He chuckled and focused on her screen and the rows of thumbnails. "These are great. Oh, look at that one. Love her expression. Hey—can you zoom in on this one?"

She double-clicked to open the photo. "Not one of my better efforts. She's not even in focus. My camera kept trying to focus on the shelves."

"Hush. Your photos are perfect. I love the soft focus behind her in the other pictures. But I'm not interested in Enolia right now. Look at the shelves behind her."

She stopped fretting about Enolia being blurry and scanned the shelves, crisply in focus with their books, knick-knacks and framed pictures. Then realization dawned. "The photos?"

"They may not tell us anything about Wayne Vandershell, but they might tell us something about her. Can you zoom in?" Alden asked.

"You're so sneaky. I love it." She zoomed in so they could look at the snapshots. One showed Enolia as a younger woman with two kids, a girl and a boy. "Does she have kids?"

"Not that I know of. So who are these two?"

"Niece? Nephew? Does she have siblings who have kids?"

Alden pulled out his phone and made a note. "I'll check. What else you got?"

Roz moved the image around on the screen. "Oh, wow. Is this who I think it is?"

Posing with Enolia at what looked like a book signing—complete with banners, a table filled with novels, and book-store shelves behind her—was a handsome, dark-haired man with brilliant white teeth. Both of them were all smiles, both holding glasses of champagne.

"That's Vandershell." Alden's voice held a note of excite-ment. "This looks cozy. How close were they? I mean, they're at a book signing, obviously. So it's not exactly a boudoir shot."

"They were business partners if he was making her movie.

But who puts a photo of their business partner on display in their living room?"

"Well, it's not in the bedroom," Alden pointed out. "Maybe she just liked the way she looks in the photo—happy, pretty and successful."

"And posing with arm candy that makes her look even more enviable."

"You think he's arm candy?" Alden's tease had the tiniest hint of jealousy.

"Not anymore! Is she that vain?" Roz thought about Enolia and her meticulous house and clothes and face. "Yeah, maybe she is. But I think there's more going on there."

"I'll try to ask her delicately." He made another note on his phone. "Any other pictures in the shot?"

Roz moved the photo around the screen some more. "Not here. Let's see if I got a different one with a focus fail."

Alden chuckled and worked on finishing off his burger. She took another bite of her sandwich and scrolled some more before she found a wider shot in which the novelist was blurry and the shelves weren't.

"Here you go," she said, zooming in until the picture was almost pixelated, sliding the image around to examine every shelf. "Here's one more. Oh my God."

Alden looked up from the fry he was pushing around in his ketchup and popped it in his mouth. "What?"

"She's at the beach in this one. Maybe even on her deck. And she's posing with someone we know." The women had their arms around each other, and both were smiling.

"Is that Mae from the bookstore?" Alden's eyes widened. "What's going on there?"

"Friends? Family? I know what you're thinking, but Mae has had a string of short-term and slightly odd boyfriends. She likes guys. I've never known her to cross the road, so to speak. Plus there's a significant age difference."

Alden shrugged. "It doesn't matter. Mae obviously knows Enolia pretty well, well enough to make the cut of the living room bookshelf. Whether she's friend or family, that would explain how our little bookstore landed Enolia Honeywood, beyond the fact she's a part-time resident of Comet Cove."

"Right. Mae had an inside connection. So Mae would know more about her, too."

"We should talk to Mae and get a quote for our Wayne Vandershell follow-up anyway," he said. "Her reaction and that sort of thing."

Roz nodded and spoke around a french fry. "In lieu of facts, color. Though I'd prefer facts."

"You always do." Alden's eyes twinkled. "That's why we make such good partners."

Roz smiled back at him. And then her phone pinged.

She looked down at the screen. "It's Duke. Maybe we can get some facts after all."

chapter
eight

ROZ PICKED up the phone and spoke quietly, not wanting other diner patrons to hear the conversation. "Duke, how's it going?"

"Hey, Roz. Sorry it's taken so long to get back to you, but I didn't have much to report, and there's still nothing official yet, OK?"

Roz tried to quell her disappointment. "Can you tell me anything, even on background?"

"You can't quote me or even say this came from the sheriff's office. And even then, I don't think you're going to be happy."

"You're killing me, Duke. What do you know? How was he killed? Shotgun?"

Whatever Duke said didn't compute.

"Wha-what?" she stammered. "Vape gun?"

"No, vape *pen*. Like those things people smoke?"

She'd misheard him the first time. But it still didn't make sense. "How did a vape pen kill him?"

"The ME thinks it exploded."

She winced as the crime scene—if it *was* a crime—popped

into her head. "So it wasn't murder, then?" She glanced up at Alden, who frowned. She shouldn't be disappointed, but she couldn't help feeling a little bit of a letdown.

"On the surface, no. Probably not."

"Wait ... *probably* not?"

Duke's voice got even lower, and since it sounded like he was in his car, that meant she really had to focus to hear him. She put a finger in the ear that wasn't glued to her phone.

"The ME and county forensics team are looking at all the evidence found at the scene. This isn't the first case of an exploding battery in a vape pen. But something looks off to them. That's all I can say for now."

"Oh, come *on*. Don't tease me."

She could almost hear Duke's grin through the phone. "Don't tease *me*," he said. "You still with that guy Alden?"

It was the first time he'd asked her directly, even though it should be obvious by now.

"I am," she said simply.

There was a beat. "OK, fair enough. We'll release something when we know more. You can say we haven't ruled out foul play. And you can attribute that to a source in the sheriff's department."

"I hate using unnamed sources, you know."

"But you will in this case, won't you? And I'll give it to you first when we know more. You find out anything about this guy?"

Ah, here was the quid pro quo. "We're still tracking it down, but we think he was planning to open a film studio here and had promised Enolia Honeywood and maybe others"—she didn't want to name Sheryl—"that he wanted to make their stories into movies."

"One of the others being Sheryl Pugh, I take it. She told me." So Duke already knew about Sheryl.

But Roz's unconscious use of "others" triggered another question in her mind.

Were there others? Other people whose dreams were crushed when Wayne met his unfortunate end?

"Roz? You still there?"

She focused on the call again. "Yeah. Thanks, Duke. Let's touch base soon."

"I appreciate any and all tips from the public. Later." He chuckled as he ended the call.

"What did he say?" Alden asked.

She decided not to tell him Duke asked about him. Alden didn't need any more grounds for teasing her. He had plenty already. "It was more what he didn't say. They haven't ruled out foul play. And the forensics people think something 'looks off' about what happened."

"But what did happen?"

"Oh, right. They said Wayne Vandershell's vape pen exploded."

"Holy cannoli." Alden grimaced. "I guess that would explain what we saw. Hard to imagine something more 'off' than a vape pen exploding."

"I can imagine a lot of things, but yeah, that seems odd to me, too. Hang on a sec." She picked up her phone again and did a quick search. "Whoa. Apparently it's not that odd— several hundred emergency room visits a year are linked to vape pen accidents, with injuries to the face, more to the hands, and most to the groin."

"The groin!" Alden said it so loudly that people at nearby tables turned their heads to look.

Roz laughed. "I guess you shouldn't carry them in your pocket."

"I don't intend to carry them at all. Ever."

"I'm so relieved. You're dangerous enough already."

He leaned in, offered a mischievous smile and pitched his voice low. "Am I?"

She whispered back. "Yes, darling. You're dangerous to my diet. I can't believe I ate this whole sandwich."

"Ha," he scoffed, sitting up straight, though his eyes twinkled.

"All right, I guess we have to go get something to put in our story." She waved over their server.

"I've got this." He pulled out his wallet. "Or I should say, *The Courier-Beacon* does."

"We can't expense every meal."

"Only the meals when we work through the story. At least until Webb calls me on it. And he won't."

"If I were in charge, reporters would pay for our own lunch." She wondered what their well-heeled publisher thought of Alden's expense reports. Not that Webb Howard, who also owned the tabloid where Alden used to work and now a network of online news sites, ever appeared in the office. She'd met him exactly once.

Alden handed a credit card to their server, who scurried away. "This is nothing compared with the bills I'd rack up at the *National Eye*. Travel, fancy restaurants, astronomical bar tabs, payoffs." He sighed. "Those were the days."

But she heard the sarcasm in his tone. "You don't miss it, do you?"

"God, no. It was awful."

She snickered.

"I'll go see Mae at the bookstore, OK?" Alden asked.

"Perfect. I'll try Nicole Esquivel first and see if she can get me an 'in' with the family. I'll try the company office if I have to, but they could give me the runaround for days. And they might want to if the project is cloaked in that much secrecy."

"*If* the movie studio is even their project," Alden said, signing the receipt the server brought back. "Let me know what you find out."

chapter
nine

DOWNTOWN COMET COVE was busier today than it was on Saturday, but Big Bang Books was a lot quieter. Last time, Alden hadn't noticed the tune that played when he opened the door, but then again, Mae had probably turned it off so it wouldn't be whistling every other second. That's what it was, a whistling tune of four notes—the call from *The Hunger Games*, he realized with amusement.

He'd donned his black sport coat so he'd look more professional, and the icy air in here made him glad of it. Light jazz filled the space. A few people browsed the shelves. The area in the back where Enolia had spoken was free of folding chairs, though a few big beanbags and armchairs now scattered there provided a comfy place to read. One beanbag had nearly swallowed a tiny lounging boy as he read *AlphaOops!* And an equally preoccupied woman—his mother?—curled up in an armchair next to him with an e-reader.

Curling up with an e-reader seemed unromantic to Alden, but he got it. He read books on his phone sometimes. Given fewer people read all the time and he was in the business of words, he was just thrilled to see someone with a bookish device in her hand.

A familiar young woman in red-framed eyeglasses read a book at the sales counter near the front, rapt. He was just wondering if he needed to ask for Mae when the owner emerged from the back hall with an armful of shiny new books and headed right for him.

"Good afternoon," she said. "I can help you in just a minute."

"No rush."

She strode past him and aimed for a display table up front, which she topped off with copies of Enolia Honeywood's *The Murex Murder*.

He wandered over. "I was here Saturday. I'm a big fan."

Mae, her purple-streaked dark hair pulled back, wore jeans and a T-shirt that said *Run As If Mr. Collins Just Proposed*. She looked up from her task. "I know you, don't I?"

"Alden Knox with *The Courier-Beacon*."

"That's right. You got a copy of her novel, didn't you?"

"I got one Saturday. And I have all her books." A handful of Enolia's other titles filled out the table.

Mae nodded, straightening the piles. "I can't keep them in stock. She's really good. But I guess if you already have your book, you're not here to buy another one?" Her smile was wary.

"You guessed right. I'm writing a follow-up story about what happened behind the store that day."

Mae looked around, nudged one more book so it aligned with the others, and sighed. "Come on back to the office. I don't want to harsh the vibe in here, you know?"

"Sure."

He followed her to the back hallway, the one that led to

the street behind the shops, then took a right turn into her windowless office. It was pretty small, but Mae seemed organized. The desk was mostly clutter-free, except for a crystal ball, a gargoyle that doubled as a pen holder, and a neat stack of papers. Filing cabinets spoke to a sense of order. But that didn't mean the space was austere. Colorful posters featured classic book covers of *Frankenstein* and *Dracula*. Special editions filled a bookcase alongside literary bric-a-brac, including a replica of the Maltese falcon and an Edgar Allan Poe bobble head. In fact, the knickknacks had a distinct spooky tone: a crocheted black bird—a raven, presumably, given Poe—along with ornate purple and black LED candles, tiny witches and wizards, and lots of skulls, many of them sparkly. They called to mind Mae's tattoos. Did she have a fascination with death? Or was she just fashionably gothic?

"Love the falcon." Alden sat in the chair in front of the desk as she sat behind it.

"Isn't it great? I love that movie. Love the book, too, but the movie is perfection."

Alden grinned. "Great to meet a fellow movie fan." Then his smile faded. "The man who died Saturday was in the movie business."

Mae nodded. "I'd heard that from Aunt Nola."

Alden's forehead wrinkled. And then it hit him. "Aunt Nola? Is she—?"

A corner of Mae's mouth lifted. "I suppose I shouldn't be outing her, but yes, Enolia Honeywood is my aunt." She suddenly looked worried. "Can you keep that out of the story?"

"I suppose it depends on whether your relationship is relevant to the story, but I understand her need for privacy and will do my best."

"That would be great. I really don't want her annoyed with me right now. Not when she's been so good to me."

Questions filled Alden's head. "Oh yeah? I want to know more about that. Do you mind if I record this, just to get the quotes right?"

Mae looked nervous, but she agreed, and he switched on his phone's recording app.

"So," he said, "I'm guessing your aunt's real last name isn't Honeywood. What is it? Just for background."

Mae swallowed. "You're not going to publish it?"

Alden gave her a reassuring smile. "How about this—I won't publish it unless it's important and it comes from another source. I think it'll be fine. OK?"

Her eyes flashed with something serious, almost angry, before she returned his smile. "OK. I'm counting on you."

"Great." Why was she so tense? "Her full name? I mean real name?"

"Nola Middleton."

Same last name as Mae. So perhaps related on her father's side. "And she's helping you out? You mean by appearing at the bookstore?"

"Oh, yeah, that helped a ton." Mae settled back in her chair, seeming more relaxed. "It's tough running a brick-and-mortar bookstore these days. We focus on community events, book clubs, everything to keep people coming back and engaged. But some months it's still hard to make the rent, and I've got a leaky roof. I love this old building, but it needs a lot of TLC. My aunt plans to make a significant investment in the shop—that's not for public consumption, by the way. Anyway, she's great."

Alden contained his frustration. Sources who declared everything off the record after it popped out of their mouths drove him crazy. It would be fun sorting out the quotes later. "She was kind to us, too. Very generous with her time. Roz and I interviewed her at her house. Beautiful place. There was a photo of you two on the bookshelves."

"You saw her house? Isn't it gorgeous? And yeah, she and I are buddies. My mom died when I was a teenager, and Aunt Nola was always the cool aunt I could talk to about things."

An image of Enolia's bookshelf popped into Alden's head. "There was another photo of her with two kids."

"Me and my brother," Mae said. "He lives in Arizona now. Not sure what this has to do with what happened Saturday, though."

"Just trying to make sure I understand the background. There was also a picture of her with Wayne Vandershell."

Mae smirked. "That was from a signing in Orlando. She told me she put it there to make her pickleball friends jealous. As if having that house and just being *her* wasn't enough."

"Was there something to be jealous of? A romantic relationship?"

"Oh, I don't think so, but Aunt Nola doesn't tell me things like that. She always has opinions on *my* love life, though." Mae rolled her eyes.

So maybe they weren't best buddies, Alden thought. He shifted in his chair, feeling all the coffee from lunch rushing through him. "So you knew Wayne, then?"

"I'd met him a few times. I knew he and my aunt were friendly. They had a business arrangement. He was a fan of hers, but he was also a movie producer and planned to turn *Shellbreak Island* into a film, possibly for streaming. If it was successful, he wanted to adapt more of her books."

"So he was going to adapt several of her books? That

sounds like a pretty big deal." And more than Enolia had told them.

"Crap, I'm talking out of turn again. You can't publish any of that without confirming it with my aunt."

Alden refrained from groaning. He had to get something on the record out of this interview. "Let's just focus on what happened Saturday. It was a great event. At least before … "

Mae looked down at her desk, reached out to touch the crystal ball. "Yeah, it was. Thanks."

"How would you describe Wayne Vandershell?"

A shadow crossed Mae's face, and then she looked up, assuming a guarded, pleasant expression.

"He was very friendly, very outgoing," she said. "He had a smile for everyone. Never met a stranger, that kind of guy."

"He had very white teeth."

Mae laughed. "He was handsome, that's for sure." Did she turn a little pink?

"Did you see him go back to the alley? The street behind the store."

Mae hesitated. "No. I don't think so. Honestly, everyone was coming and going to the bathrooms, and I was focused on my little speech and keeping my aunt happy, which wasn't easy."

"Why not?"

"She seemed nervous. And she's not usually that way, not before an appearance. She's more introspective out of the spotlight, but she has a gift for turning on her personality when she steps on stage. Or whatever you want to call a book signing. She'd forgotten the book she'd marked up for the reading, and I had to give her another one. That kind of thing."

"Did she say anything about Wayne before or after the—the incident?"

Mae frowned. "No, nothing. She was totally focused on the event. She was fussing about some tiny stain on her dress. I gave her my brooch to wear over it. Oh my gosh. Don't print anything about that or about her being nervous, please. Why are you asking all these questions? Was he—was he really murdered? Deputy Byrd told me it was probably an accident."

Did she, now? Usually Naya Byrd wouldn't give him the time of day. "The police don't seem to be sure what happened yet." And he was getting nowhere, especially if Mae kept telling him not to publish what she told him. He could respect her wishes to a point, given he was mostly here to get color, but he had to get *something* and get going. "How would you describe the general mood after it happened?"

"Well, people were concerned, of course. It was all very shocking. But I have to say, my aunt is a pro. And absolutely quote me on that. She was very empathetic and talked to the audience for a few minutes before she signed books. She didn't do her reading. She didn't do her usual funny stuff. But she was so kind to everyone, they relaxed. She really took the stress out of the room."

And they bought more books. Well, he did, anyway, but Roz had asked him to.

"She was very professional," he agreed.

"I'm hoping she'll come back and do another event."

Alden perked up. "Really? Soon?"

"We haven't settled on the details." She sensed his impatience. "I'll let you know as soon as I know, all right? We'd love to have a story in the paper."

One not focused on a potential murder, he thought. "That

would be great. Anything else you want to tell me about what happened Saturday?"

"Only that I really appreciate the police and emergency services for getting here so fast. They're wonderful."

Small-town heroes. Check. He stood, grabbing his phone. "Thanks for taking the time. If I have any more questions, I might give you a call."

Mae blinked and stood, too. "That's fine. Tell Roz I said hi."

"Will do." He exited the office first, sheepishly pointed to the restrooms, and ducked into one as she headed out to the main floor.

A couple of minutes later, feeling much better, he found himself in the hallway. And drawn back to the scene of the crime. Or the vape. Whatever it was.

With a look over his shoulder, he headed down the dim hallway toward the back door and pushed it open into a bright afternoon. The rain had gone, though the pavement still looked wet in spots. He let the door ease shut but propped it open with a brick that lay next to the door, probably there for just that purpose, for deliveries and so on.

The alley was mostly empty, though there were a few vehicles behind the various businesses that backed up to the street on each side. All the vehicles were parallel-parked on one side since it was one-way. Any evidence of what had happened was gone. No debris. And the rain had probably washed away anything else. He didn't want to think about that.

Big Bang Books was in the middle of a block. He looked both ways, toward the cross streets at each end of the alley, where the occasional car passed by. They were pretty far away. It was unlikely there would be rolling witnesses. He scanned the businesses, looking for cameras. There was one a few doors down, but it was focused on the back door of that building. No help.

Surely the police had thought of all that. Just as they'd looked in the dumpster a couple of doors down.

Or had they?

It was dark green, with black lids on the top that looked easy enough to lift. He'd just take a quick look. The businesses here shared it, he figured.

Alden reached the dumpster, looked around and didn't spot any witnesses. Then he lifted one of the two lids and peeked inside. It didn't smell good, but the bagged trash didn't seem that unusual, and he had one rule when it came to reporting, even when he was with the *National Eye*: He did *not* go dumpster-diving. After all, Wayne Vandershell died when his vape pen exploded. It wasn't like somebody dropped a gun or a knife in here.

He took a step back and spotted a recycling bin next to the trash container. It was a little bigger than the rolling trash cans outside his apartment, but bright green and painted with a white recycling symbol. It had been hidden from view when he was down the street. What the heck, he thought.

He lifted the lid and saw a jumble of soda cans, a few bottles, various papers, and—a book?

He thought he recognized the cover, though he could see only the back of it. It was half covered with papers.

Did his rule against dumpster-diving apply to recycling bins?

Alden didn't have to dive. The bin wasn't that big. He reached in and flipped the book so he could see the front of it.

It was Enolia Honeywood's *The Murex Murder*.

A jolt ran through him. Who would've thrown out a brand-new book?

He looked around the pavement, found a thin plastic grocery bag that had escaped the trash but was still reasonably clean, and used it to pluck the book out of the recycling. Then he got the book inside the bag without adding any more of his fingerprints, just in case, and squeezed it into the inside pocket of his jacket. He headed back toward the bookshop.

He'd just moved inside and eased the door closed when Mae appeared out of the gloom.

"Alden?"

"Oh, hi, Mae. I just wanted to look around outside to—you know. See the scene again."

"Are you done?" Her tone was courteous, but it was clear she was ready for him to go. That was OK. He was ready, too. And he wanted to look at the book he'd found.

"Yes, thanks." But another question occurred to him as he followed her into the main room of the store and toward the front door. "Hey, Mae? Who took that photo of you and your aunt at her house?"

"Oh, that was Craig." She rolled her eyes. "He's always around. He lives above her garage."

chapter
ten

ROZ DIDN'T HAVE Nicole Esquivel's number. She'd called April Reins from the parking lot behind the diner and boardwalk and left a voicemail. April texted her back a few minutes later, saying she didn't have Nicole's personal cell but Liani Reyes might. A few more minutes of phone tag, and Roz had it.

She would've preferred just dropping in, but she figured she'd be less intimidating if she cleared the runway first.

Nicole answered after three rings. "Hello?" she said over a cacophony of music and screams in the background.

"Hi, Nicole? This is Roz Melander. We met at the book signing on Saturday."

"Roz. Of course, Roz! You almost got drafted into babysitting. Sorry about that."

Roz chuckled. "I wouldn't have minded for five minutes. Anything longer than that, we'd have to negotiate. Besides, I'm way out of practice."

"Be careful what you volunteer for! Teens are so busy these days, it's hard to find one free on a Saturday. I'm always looking." Her voice dropped in volume as she apparently held the phone away from her mouth. "Gabriela! Stop screeching and turn down the TV! I don't want Diego to wake up!" Then she was back to Roz. "Sorry about that. I just got him asleep, and she's all wound up after VPK. What can I do for you?"

"I work for the paper, as I think you know, and I have some questions you or your husband might be able to help me with. Do you think I could drop by?"

Nicole waited a moment to answer. "Can you tell me what this is about?"

"Sure. We're trying to figure out who might be doing a construction project by the airport and thought someone in the Esquivel family might know. I immediately thought of you." That was good, Roz thought. Truthful but vague—acknowledging Nicole as a valuable source—and no mention of a possible murder.

"OK." Nicole's reply held a note of relief. "Seb is working from home today. You might as well come over."

Roz wondered how anyone could work with that din—the TV and screeching only slightly less loud than before—but she jumped on the offer, got the address and was soon driving toward Saturn Shores, one of the nicer southside neighborhoods. She glimpsed a few of its waterfront houses as she crossed the bridge over Star Inlet. Saturn Shores' most palatial homes loomed on the curving shoreline where the inlet met the Indian River Lagoon.

A couple of canals also cut into the neighborhood, ensuring maximum properties with boat access to the river. During the holidays, a boat parade started at Southside Wharf, a bit south of Saturn Shores, then crawled up the lagoon and through the canals before dipping into the inlet and ending up at Star Harbor on the north side. It was good cheesy fun, the boats sparkling with colorful strings of lights and people picnicking and partying along every waterway. It was also several months off, Roz reminded herself, and they had summer and hurricane season to get through before the delights of Florida's winter returned.

She was still damp from the spring shower that had doused her—April rains indeed—so she took a quick detour south to her neighborhood, made a Clark-Kent-worthy speed change into a black V-neck and jeans, and tamed and put up her hair. Then she was back on the road, heading to the home of Nicole and Sebastian Esquivel.

Saturn Shores had a gatehouse, but it hadn't held a guard in some time, and no gate stood in her way. At some point, the homeowners' association had given up on the extra cost of security. She'd written recently about their plan to bring it back, prompted by the celebrities buying into the place. Though mostly, security people for these upmarket enclaves seemed to spend their days waving through service vehicles, not stopping home invaders.

Guided by the GPS on her phone, Roz wound through impeccably landscaped, rococo McMansions with big front yards, paver driveways and hints of hidden screened-in pools. The lucky ones backed up to canals or the lagoon. Most of them were at least two stories, presumably to take advantage of the views and, of course, maximize the square footage.

The Esquivels' stucco home, two stories with a steep roof and a jumble of jutting pseudo-wings and architectural adornments, was painted a subtle cream color and trimmed in white. Even its barrel-tile roof matched the light colors, saving energy by reflecting Florida's heat. Or maybe someone just thought it was pretty.

Roz parked in the wide driveway, which ran to a large attached garage and a side door. It was probably the door the family used most, but she figured she'd better hike the mile-long sidewalk around the front of the house to the main entrance. She skirted a great deal of extravagant tropical landscaping before she got there.

The entryway was recessed under an arched overhang. The double doors were of dark carved wood. Into each were inset frosted, leaded glass crescents that mirrored each other, creating a split circle. The package screamed "successful housing developer who could afford top wholesale prices."

Suitably impressed, Roz found the camera doorbell on the wall and pressed the button. A complex Westminster-level chime sounded beyond the door, though she didn't hear any screaming as she had on the phone. That was a good sign.

Nicole didn't answer the door, but a pleasant, good-looking guy—tan with dark hair and eyes and a bit of a dad bod—did. He wore a white golf shirt, plaid shorts and boat shoes, and he smiled when he saw her. "You must be Roz."

"Yes, I am. Mr. Esquivel?"

"Sebastian, please. Come on in."

The round two-story entrance hall held a sweeping staircase that curved up one wall, a central round marble table sporting a towering fake flower arrangement, and a tiny plastic tricycle in bright yellow and blue. At least someone was using all this floor space for fun.

Roz shook off the nerves she always felt meeting someone new. "Thanks for taking the time. I thought Nicole might greet me."

"She figured I could help you, so she's taken Gabby next door to play with a friend while Diego takes a nap. This is about as quiet as it gets." A corner of his mouth lifted. "Once Mateo gets home from kindergarten, all bets are off."

Roz chuckled. "Not a problem. I won't take that long."

"Fine. How about we go to my office?" He turned away suddenly and sneezed loudly into his arm. "Sorry. My allergies are the devil right now."

"Bless you." What else could she say?

A minute later, after a track up the stairs and through a mini maze of hallways, they entered a room that felt like the inside of a small barn, with sloped gable walls on the sides. A sectional couch lined one of those walls, facing an entertainment center with a TV the size of an aircraft carrier. A small bar was tucked in an alcove in one corner by the door. Now this was an office!

Against the wall with the door, a vintage pinball machine glowed. Its back glass featured cartoon baseball players and a blinking blimp and said "BIG HIT." Hanging on the wall all around the machine (and the door) were signed collectibles: photos, baseball cards, a leather glove and baseballs in shadow boxes. The centerpiece was a Tampa Bay Rays jersey covered in autographs.

"Would I be making an assumption to say you like baseball?" Roz asked.

Sebastian laughed. "Is it that obvious? I played in the minors for a year before I joined the family business and then got kind of obsessed with collecting. I'm nuts about the Rays. Their time will come."

"I'm sure it will." Roz had no notion of the Rays' record, but she respected a loyal fan. "That's so cool. I love pinball machines." She gestured toward the blinking BIG HIT.

"Want to play?"

Duty called, much to Roz's regret. "Better not. Then I might start having fun."

"Right," he said. "You're working. Let's go out to the balcony. Would you like something to drink?"

"No, I'm good."

He went behind the bar and got a bottle of water for himself from a fridge there, then guided her past a large, neat wooden desk that faced the French doors, which he opened for her. Outside, they settled into comfortable cushioned chairs and took a moment to look over the screened pool cage and the dock and the big boat there. Midafternoon sunlight played on the lagoon. She couldn't quite see the inlet from here, but she knew it was just to the north.

"Sweet view."

"I know. I'm lucky." Sebastian turned to her. "So what can I do for you?"

She pulled a notebook from her bag and opened it to a blank page, scribbling the date and his name at the top. "We've heard some rumors—"

"We?" he asked.

"We. *The Courier-Beacon.* And the reporter I'm working with, Alden Knox."

"All right. Go on."

"We've heard rumors that a movie studio is in the works near the airport and thought you might know who's behind it, since your family has had a lot of real estate dealings in that area."

He blinked. "Seriously?"

"Um, yes." Was she totally on the wrong track?

"I was assured the project would remain quiet until we were ready to announce it. And yet here you are."

Bingo! Roz tried not to sound too excited. "So it's your project? Why did you want to keep it quiet?"

He sighed and looked out at the water again. "I didn't want to keep it quiet, but my partner did. He wanted to have some film deals to announce first. Wanted us to get started on the construction. Of course, he was the source of all our delays."

"Wayne Vandershell, you mean?"

Sebastian snapped his gaze back to her, his mouth slightly open. "How on earth?"

"How do we know? He wasn't keeping it quiet. The movie studio, I mean. He told one of our correspondents about it and said he had a partner, though he didn't mention you."

"But you found me anyway."

"Just lucky." Luck and her mom's insight. "Are you willing to talk about it?"

"Of course. I didn't see the need for all the secrecy, but he said it was a Hollywood thing. And now that he's dead, honestly, I'm not sure what's next." He pulled a handkerchief from his pocket and blew his nose, then stowed it. "Pollen. Blech."

Roz suppressed a smile. "Can you give me any details on your arrangement with Mr. Vandershell?"

"Well, for one thing, it's not the kind of project I usually do. Or have ever done. A movie studio? But it seemed like a pretty cool thing to bring to Comet Cove." He hesitated. He wasn't telling her everything.

"So you were going to build it for him and he was going to run it?"

"He was going to run it, yes, but we were financial partners. And the contract was pretty loose. I guess I got caught up in all his talk. He said he was lining up projects and investors. That Blake Burbage would star in one of his movies. That kind of thing. There were parts of our deal that weren't on paper, which I came to regret. But I had my reasons."

Roz took a couple of notes. "We've all had regrets. Are you talking about the delays you mentioned?"

"Delays related to money. We were supposed to be part-ners, but he didn't deliver on his end of the deal, and I wasn't going to foot the whole bill myself. The permits were in the works, but the financing wasn't there. He kept putting me off or dropping just enough for me to buy supplies piecemeal."

"Why didn't you walk away?"

"It was my property—a piece my mother had given me. The warehouses were old and hadn't been used in years, and I was trying to decide what to do with it. Once we got started on the studio construction, I hesitated to back out, and the agreement, however weak, would have made it difficult to do so without paying off Wayne. That's the irony, given he hadn't held up his end of the deal."

"But you had other reasons for persisting with the movie studio project?" Roz prodded.

Sebastian took a sip from his water bottle. "Listen, I don't care if you write about the studio, even though my family will give me crap about it. But if I tell you this part, I don't want it in the paper."

OK, Roz thought. *I can always try to talk him into going on the record later.*

She made a show of putting her notebook down on her lap. "I'd like to know. And I'll keep it out of the paper."

"He'd agreed to produce Nicki's screenplay. It's always been a dream of hers, and she spends so much time being a mom that writing is kind of her only escape. She's done pitchfests and contests and has never gotten anywhere. But she ran into Wayne at a book club at Big Bang Books, and she introduced us. He told me about wanting to create a movie studio here, and we made a deal. I'd help him create the studio, and he'd make her movie."

Roz kept her face neutral, but inside, she buzzed. Another

writer whose dreams were shattered by Wayne's death. Or was Wayne using Nicole to get to Sebastian? "Does Nicole know?"

He shook his head. "No. She doesn't know that's why I agreed to do the project. But she was really upset about his death. I was supposed to pick up the kids Saturday at the bookstore so she could enjoy Enolia Honeywood's signing, and I had a delay at a construction site that made me late. By the time I pulled in, she was hysterical, and the kids were all freaking out."

Roz thought back to Saturday. Nicole had taken the kids to the restroom. She'd come out looking rough, but who could blame her, wrangling three little kids? Then there was the scream—Sheryl—and she and Alden had run out back. She never saw Nicole after that. The harried mom must have heard about Wayne and left.

"Saturday was crazy," Roz conceded. "Do you think Wayne was serious about making Nicole's movie?"

"Good question. Now that I know what I know, I don't think much of Wayne Vandershell." Sebastian's voice was low and civilized, but it had a dark and angry undertone that scared her a little. "And I don't think he always told the truth."

Roz let that sit for a minute, then picked up her notebook. If Wayne's death was a murder—she really needed to get more out of Duke—could Sebastian have had something to do with it? Maybe he happened upon Wayne in the alley when no one was looking. But she couldn't ask him that point-blank. Not yet.

"Do you intend to go forward with the movie studio project?"

He shook his head. "Probably not. Not unless I get another backer. I just don't know the business. We've done some work with wiring and structures, and it would be a shame for it to go to waste, but I'll probably have to pivot. It's just hard to imagine, say, an industrial park with a suburban street facade built in the middle of it."

Roz's eyes widened. "You got that far along?"

"Wayne wanted something we could show other investors. We completed part of it on my dime. Most people film on location now, don't they? But he really wanted the look of it. Now I wonder why."

So did Roz. "Maybe if he couldn't come up with the money, he wanted other people to."

"I suppose so, but he hadn't brought any visitors by, as far as I know. Or maybe he did, but he didn't tell me. And if he got any investments, I never saw the money."

"I'd love to see what you built. Maybe get a few pictures?" Any elements of a movie set would make great photos for the paper. Even better if it was only half built.

Sebastian seemed to relax a little. "Why not? Maybe it'll get another investor interested."

Yes! "I'd like to bring my colleague along. And maybe our photographer, though it might be me shooting the photos."

"That's fine. Call me later today and we'll set it up. I need to ask my assistant what's on my schedule."

"Great. Thanks for giving me some time today." Roz packed away her notebook as Sebastian stood, and they exchanged business cards in his office. They went downstairs and reached the front door just as a ruckus sounded from an unseen room.

"That'll be Nicki and the kids coming in through the kitchen. She was going to pick up Mateo at the bus stop."

"Daaaaaad!" The little boy's yell preceded his breathless arrival on wee running feet.

"Mateo!" Sebastian swept the boy up, ruffled his dark hair,

and gave him a hug and a kiss on the cheek. Then he set him down. "Do you know Ms. Melander?"

"Roz. I'm Roz," she told Mateo. "We met on Saturday, sort of."

Mateo eyed her.

Sebastian headed off toward the noise. "I'm going to see if Nicki needs help. Talk to you later. Mateo, come get your snack."

"OK, Dad." The boy stood still, though, looking shyly at Roz. "Are you Mommy's friend?"

"Yes, I'm a new friend of your mom's. We both went to the book signing on Saturday."

"Mommy took me to the bathroom and Gabby came too because she didn't want to stay with you."

Roz guffawed. "That seems to be the case."

"I'm old enough to go by myself, but Mommy always wants to come." He rolled his eyes. "But she told me to watch the *little* kids when she left for a couple of minutes. That's because I'm the oldest."

"Wow. She did? That must mean you're very mature for your age."

"Mateo!" Nicole's voice called from the kitchen.

"Yes, I am *mature*." He enounced the word like it was new to him and beamed. "I have to go before Gabby eats all of my cookies." And off he ran.

But as she let herself out the front door, Roz was still stuck on "Wow." Nicole left her kids in the bathroom on Saturday while she disappeared. Where did she go?

Did she go see Wayne Vandershell?

ALDEN TOOK a sip of his black brew and regarded his laptop. He'd typed up a very rough draft of a story that left out way more than it said. And he needed to know what Roz got before they could publish anything. He picked up his phone to text her.

> How'd it go with the Esquivels?

She responded a few minutes later.

> We should talk.

> Let's meet.

> Bean Me Up?

> Already there.

> Of course you are. 😏 See you in ten.

He had time to order her a mocha before she arrived; this time of the afternoon, there were only a couple of people at separate tables, wrapped up in their computers. The big windows filled the place with afternoon light that made the space art glow, and a mix of folk and alternative rock played over the speakers.

The door jingled as Roz rolled in, wearing a different outfit from what she'd had on at lunch. Whatever she wore, she made his heart fizz. She strolled over to his table in the back corner, which sat under a big streak shot of a nighttime rocket launch. He stood and kissed her on the cheek.

"I missed you," Alden told Roz.

"You've been too busy to miss me." She plunked her bag on the floor and sat in the chair next to his.

"That's your answer?" he said as he settled in his chair.

She gave him a shy look. "I missed you, too." She eyed the paper cup he pushed toward her. "Do I smell mocha? You're the best." She scooped it up and took a long sip.

Alden eyed her with skepticism. "How is it that I am the more sentimental one in this relationship? I'm the cynic."

"Are you still a cynic?"

"Sometimes," he admitted.

"Cynics are basically idealists who are jaded by a world that doesn't share their values. Which is the standard journalist headspace," Roz said.

"Cynics are also broken romantics."

"That too. Which are you?"

"Both." He slipped one hand behind her neck, leaned in and covered her mouth with his. He lingered in the kiss, tasting her sweetness, feeling her respond. Coffee and chocolate and heat.

They parted, and Roz made a little whimpering sound. And let out a sigh.

He could hear her make those sounds all day. Or all night.

He grinned, expecting a lecture about public displays of affection, but she just looked up at him under her eyelashes with a coy half smile before she reached down to dig her computer out of her bag.

"Are you writing?" she asked, nodding at his open laptop on the table.

"Trying to draft some kind of story. It's not easy. Mae told me a lot but kept asking me to keep it off the record. I only have a few bland nuggets about Wayne's personality and Enolia being awesome. And guess what? Enolia is her aunt."

"What? For real?"

"For real," Alden said. "That's one reason Enolia did a signing in our little town. And Mae—who says hi, by the way—told me Enolia promised to invest in the bookshop, which needs cash. She didn't say it was a dire situation, but that was the impression I got."

"And Mae knew Wayne?"

"A little. She said he was likable and handsome. She might've even gotten a little flustered when she said that, but I could be imagining things."

Roz stared at Alden. "Do you think she had a thing for Wayne Vandershell?"

"I don't know. What did you get from the Esquivels? Did you find Wayne's partner?"

Roz's face lit up. "Sebastian Esquivel didn't just direct me to Wayne Vandershell's partner—he *is* the partner. Or was."

"No kidding. And they were working on a movie studio?"

Roz nodded. "But they didn't get that far, partly because Wayne wasn't meeting his financial obligations. Though apparently he had hopes of raising money to make the project go forward. They even built part of an outdoor set to entice potential investors, though Sebastian never saw any come through. He said he would show us around and we can take photos."

Alden smirked. "That's awfully nice of him."

"Your cynicism is showing. You think he's being open about the studio so we won't look into other things?"

"I distrust anything that's so easy. But I'm willing to go."

"Good. I'll contact him in a bit to see when we can do it." A tiny wrinkle formed in her brow. "And this is kind of weird, but when Nicole took her kids to the bathroom prior to Enolia's signing, apparently she left them all in there alone for a few minutes while she disappeared. I'm wondering where she went."

"Who told you that?"

"The oldest boy, who's only about five. I know, not a reliable source."

Alden crossed his arms and leaned back, thinking. "So she could've gone to see Wayne? Why?"

"I don't know. I hope it wasn't for romantic reasons. Sebastian seemed like a nice guy. Except he got pretty angry talking about Wayne. And I think part of the reason is Nicole. And this part was off the record—"

"Of course it was."

Roz chuckled. "I know. Anyway, Wayne promised to produce Nicole's screenplay if Sebastian agreed to the movie studio deal, which apparently wasn't the best contract Sebastian ever signed. He didn't want to tell her that's why he agreed to partner up with Wayne. He was just trying to make her dream come true."

All of this skulduggery hurt Alden's head. "Did you ask her whether she went to see Wayne in back of the bookstore Saturday morning?"

"No. She was busy with the kids, and my interview with Sebastian was over. I want to know more before I bring it up."

"So you haven't talked to Duke again?"

"Ooo, good point." She took another sip of her mocha, then dredged her phone out of her bag and tapped the screen. She held it to her ear, and Alden got to hear very little of the conversation, with Roz's short answers and questions and Duke inaudible. But her eyebrows seemed to lift higher with every answer.

By the time she finished the call, he couldn't contain his curiosity. "Tell me."

She set the phone on the table and looked around to make sure no one was too close. Then she leaned in and spoke low. "We can't publish this yet, but that vape pen didn't just explode. One, they think the battery was tampered with."

"Whoa." Alden leaned in, too. "So it's murder?"

"Or at least malice aforethought. And they found marks on the body that indicated he'd probably been struck on the head and arms. Bruises and cuts. Maybe a fight. Maybe defensive wounds."

"Okaaaay ... and that means what? He was attacked by the same person who sabotaged the vape pen?"

"Maybe," she said. "Maybe not. He might've gotten in a scuffle before he even showed up at the signing. But I wonder —if the vape pen was somehow damaged in a fight, would that have hastened its demise?"

"And Wayne's?" Alden said.

"Could be. Fight aside, damaging the vape pen's battery with the intention to cause harm—I'm not even sure what charge that would be, but it sure looks like murder."

"Poor Wayne. If only it had been his groin."

Roz laughed, then covered her mouth. "You're so bad."

"That's why you like me. So we're looking for a killer and also maybe someone else who hit him and hurried things along."

"I guess we are. They could be one and the same person. Someone was very, very angry with Wayne Vandershell."

"Oh!" Alden exclaimed. "I almost forgot to tell you—I was nosing around the crime scene, or whatever it was, and found one of Enolia's books in the recycling bin. Her new one. I had to borrow some gloves from Lily"—Alden nodded at the counter, where the barista was filling an order—"just to make sure I didn't contaminate it."

"Are you saying this is evidence? If it is, we need to give it to Duke."

"Will you quit sucking up to Duke?"

She laughed. "He gave us some good details."

"That we can't publish."

"We can still say a source at the sheriff's office says foul play may be involved. So what's the story with the book?"

"You can give it to Duke," Alden said grudgingly. He reached under the table and pulled up the book, now in a clean zip-lock bag (also thanks to Lily). "I looked at it earlier. It's Enolia Honeywood's brand-new novel."

"I can see that."

A corner of his mouth lifted. "Yes, except it doesn't look brand-new. It looks, shall we say, used. Scuffed around the edges. Dirty. And there are sticky notes and highlighted pages in it."

"Maybe somebody liked to take notes when they were reading but didn't want to keep it when they were done. Is it signed?"

Alden shook his head. "I think this is Enolia's copy."

Roz sat up. "How so?"

"Mae told me Enolia forgot her marked-up copy and had to borrow another one for the reading. I think this is the marked-up copy."

"So how did it end up in the recycling bin? Did someone steal it? Or did she put it there?"

"That's something we're going to have to find out," Alden said. "So who do we talk to next? Before we talk to Enolia again, of course. And Craig, her assistant. Mae says he lives above her garage. He has to know where all the bodies are buried, so to speak."

"I agree we should learn more before we talk to her again," Roz said. "Sebastian gave me another lead. Wayne apparently told him he planned to put Blake Burbage into a movie."

"Did he now?" Alden smiled. "I love talking to movie stars. And now Blake and I are buddies."

"After ten minutes of chatting at the book signing?"

"We men are shallow. We don't need a deep conversation to be friends."

Roz snorted. "Sounds about right. Are you friendly enough to have his phone number?"

Alden winced. "Well ..."

"Maybe one of those other guys he was with has his number."

Alden thought for a moment. "Yeah. One was a golf pro at Vesper Lakes. He's given me dish before. Let me try him."

"Great. And I'll ping Sebastian. And then we'll write something up for the web so John's head doesn't explode."

chapter
twelve

"HE ACTUALLY TOLD us to come over!" Alden set down his phone after a flurry of calls, looking as surprised as if someone had just slapped him.

Roz had to laugh. He was just so cute sometimes. "What, you doubted your new best buddy, Blake Burbage?"

After filing a short article for John that mentioned the possibility of foul play, a few details about the movie studio deal and some color from Mae, they hit the road in Alden's Miata. Roz left her car in front of the newspaper's office just down the street.

She insisted they stop by the sheriff's department. Deputies Duke Dawson and Naya Byrd were out, but she left the book for Duke with a note.

"Did you leave him doughnuts, too?" Alden snarked as she climbed back into his sporty little car.

She smiled. "Maybe next time."

Alden grumbled, but she was pretty sure he did it just to nag her, in a pigtail-pulling kind of way. She kind of liked that he was jealous, even if he was just teasing her. Nobody had ever cared that much before.

Her phone pinged on their way to the beach and Enolia Honeywood's neighborhood. She glanced at the text. "It's Sebastian Esquivel. He says we can meet him at the studio site at five."

Alden glanced at the clock on the dash. "Will we make it?"

"I think so. Depends on if Blake invites you to a sleepover."

"Oh, shut up." But his eyes twinkled and his mouth twitched, halfway to a smile.

Blake Burbage also had a gate, but he answered the intercom himself before he buzzed them in.

A mini forest of palms partly obscured his house from the road, but the building stuck up so high it was easy to see most of it. At three stories with a cupola—with most of the lower floor taken up by a garage with two wide doors—it was tall and relatively narrow compared with Enolia's place. But as they parked next to it, Roz could see the building had plenty of depth. This was another big house, with riotous siding in sunflower yellow and turquoise with white accents.

"Boy, my place is going to feel really small when I go home tonight," she said as they got out of the car.

"You could always come to my apartment first. Then when you go to your house, it will seem bigger," Alden joked.

She chuckled. "You're not wrong."

The main door was on the side of the house, nestled in a recess under a balcony.

Blake Burbage answered the doorbell in bare feet, navy shorts and an "I Love My Shih Tzu" T-shirt with a goofy-looking dog on it. Rushing down the steps behind him was the dog itself, probably a girl given the froufrou pink ribbons in her long white and gray fur. The tiny pup-mop bounced up and down on her front feet as she yapped.

"Calm down, Morgana," Blake said, running a hand through his not-quite-short silver-streaked dark hair. He still looked good, fiftysomething or not. He bent down and ruffled the dog's head, and the barking subsided to a low growl. "She probably won't bite you."

"Great," Alden said wryly. "Thanks for letting us stop by. This is Roz Melander."

"Roz." Blake broke into a beaming smile and fixed her with his bright blue eyes, and her heart stopped for a minute. Yes, he *really* looked good.

"H-h-hi." She hated herself for the nerves, but she didn't meet movie stars every day. She stuck out her hand, and he shook it, and then everything was normal again.

"You have to come up the stairs unless you want to take the elevator in the garage," he said.

"No problem," Alden replied, and they trudged up the steep staircase, led by the pitter-patter of Morgana's tiny feet.

This thing needs a ski lift, Roz thought as they made it to the second floor. Its large, open, light-filled space stretched all the way past dining and living areas to the sliding glass doors, balcony and views of the sea.

She wandered close enough to the glass to see the pool below and more balconies above as the dog danced around her feet. She reached down and scratched under the pup's chin before taking another look at the sparkling blue ocean. "Spectacular view."

"It really is," Blake agreed. "And for this I paid less than half of what I got for my beach house in California."

"Morgana!" came a lilting voice from down a hallway. "Treats!" The dog lost all interest in Roz and took off running.

"Lexie loves that dog. She gave me this ridiculous shirt," Blake said with an indulgent smile. Roz had no idea who Lexie was, but Alden nodded knowingly. Obviously someone famous enough for her gossip guy to recognize.

Alden looked around at the modern furniture and tasteful accents, homing in on a credenza against one wall topped with unusual objects.

Roz followed and halted before a familiar sight. "Oh, wow, is this that cowbell that was on your desk in *Chain of Honor?*"

Blake grinned. "Good eye."

"I loved that show." She could hear herself gushing but couldn't help it. "I loved every time you rang the cowbell to pull Doberman from his latest distraction."

The star looked pleased. "The bell was my idea."

Alden leaned over to look at a small glass box. "That's not the compass button from *Flameout*, is it? Oh my God."

"It sure is. Do you want to hold it?"

Alden could barely gasp out a yes, and Roz could barely hide her amusement. It was so rare to see him act like a fanboy. Blake lifted away the clear box and set it aside, leaving only the black display base, and picked up what looked like an ordinary brass button—until he unscrewed it to reveal a tiny compass. He handed it to Alden, who gently rolled it around on his palm before handing it back.

"It works, too," Blake said. "If you got shot down like I did in the movie, you could remove the button and use this with a silk map sewn into your uniform to find your way to safety."

"That's amazing," Roz said. "They really used those in World War II?"

"They sure did." Blake lowered the glass case over the button. "That's one thing I loved about working on that movie. The authenticity. I loved the history and all the war gadgets. And I love to fly, so I geeked out over all the aviation stuff."

"I didn't know you were a pilot. That's cool," Alden said.

"I've got a Beechcraft Bonanza over at Comet Cove International."

They all chuckled at this reference to the small airfield, which hadn't graduated to international flights yet. At least not officially.

Blake gestured them toward a seating area of soft beige furniture where they had an excellent view of the ocean. They took a couch; he took a chair. Alden didn't ask to record as he usually did, so she got out her notebook and pen.

Blake saw her do it but didn't seem concerned. "So what can I do for you two? I saw your latest story on poor Wayne. Foul play, eh?"

Wow, John worked fast. He must've liked what they wrote to get the article online already.

And Blake had just called Wayne by his first name.

Alden beat her to the obvious question. "You knew Wayne Vandershell?"

"I did. He was trying to talk me into starring in an indie movie. He described it as 'offbeat.' He kept saying I'd have a comeback like John Travolta in *Pulp Fiction*." His mouth quirked. "I wasn't sure whether to be flattered or insulted that he assumed I needed a 'comeback.' I'm very happy here." But there was something in Blake's face that made Roz wonder.

"You weren't tempted?" she asked.

"Of course I was tempted. I'm starting to get a few scripts to look at again since my role in that creepy priest film. Small roles in horror movies and that kind of thing. I haven't taken one yet, but that doesn't mean I won't. I always think of Ray Milland—you know his work?"

"Great actor," Alden said.

"He was. Won the Oscar for *The Lost Weekend*. He had a lot of great roles, big roles."

"I loved him in Hitchcock's *Dial M for Murder*." Alden brimmed with enthusiasm while Roz made a mental note to catch up on her classic movies.

"Oh, he was great at being evil," Blake agreed. "And then almost twenty years after *The Lost Weekend*, he was starring in *The Man with the X-Ray Eyes*. I mean, it wasn't terrible. It's Roger Corman. But it was pretty cheesy stuff. I don't mind pulp if I have a good role. But I was still waiting for Wayne to show me the script that would herald my triumphant return." He shrugged. "Can't say easy come, easy go, because I never saw it to begin with."

Roz saw a theme here. "So he promised you something but didn't deliver?"

Blake regarded her with those sharp blue eyes. "He was careful not to promise anything. He talked a good game. Why he wasn't in Hollywood, I'll never understand." It was a joke, but his smile thinned. Was he angry under all the good cheer? He'd really wanted that comeback script.

"Did you know he was planning to build a movie studio by the airport?" Alden asked.

"Of course. He considered it part of the glorious cinema-fication of Comet Cove."

"He told his construction partner you were on board with doing a movie there," Roz said.

"Did he now?" Blake's eyebrows rose, and there was a flash of something like hope immediately dashed by reality in his face. As if he thought: *The movie's happening ... no, wait. The producer's dead.*

There was a pause before Alden asked, "Were you familiar with his previous work?"

"I looked it up online, but no, I hadn't heard of those movies. Of course, I can't keep up with everything nowadays. Streaming. YouTube. Everybody's famous," he said dryly. "Have you seen any of it?"

"No. I'm too busy watching Turner Classic Movies."

Blake made an amused sound and gave Alden a keen look. "You're too modest. I'd say you're right on top of current events." In other words, he knew exactly who Alden was and wanted him to know he knew.

There was a beat, and Roz saw an opportunity. "Did you see Wayne when you went into the back hallway at the bookstore Saturday during the event with Enolia Honeywood?"

Blake shifted in his chair and turned to her. "Oh, that's right. You were there, weren't you?"

"Yes. Alden's a big fan," Roz said.

"She's good, isn't she?" Blake replied. But the blasé way he said it made her wonder if he knew the answer. Had he read Enolia's books?

"So did you see Wayne?" she pushed.

Blake nodded once. "I saw him come in, exchanged a hello. He disappeared, and I never saw him again."

He disappeared because you killed him and then you never saw him again? she thought. Or maybe her imagination was getting ahead of her.

After a moment, Alden filled the awkward silence. "That was an enthusiastic crowd."

Blake seemed to relax a bit. "Yeah, I wish they'd come to see me."

They all laughed, and it felt like the interview was over. Alden must've felt the same, because he stood. "Thanks so much for your time."

"No problem." Blake stood as well, regarding him evenly.

"You know I have a reputation for shooting from the hip, and I don't mean in my movies. I don't need a publicist to manage everything I say."

Alden nodded as Roz wondered where Blake was going.

"But I know you'll use good judgment when you decide what to write after our chat today," the actor continued. "I'd love to talk to you again when I have some news."

Oh, he was good. *Treat me well, and I'll give you access.* He was someone who knew how to use his fame and the power it gave him.

"I'm not in the gotcha business anymore," Alden said, returning Blake's frankness. "But I'm in the business of publishing the truth." *Go, Alden!* "And I'd love to talk to you and Lexie sometime."

Blake smiled. "Until then." They shook hands.

Whoa, that was slick. But she could live with their deal. The paper would publish the truth, wherever it led them, but a little discretion didn't hurt.

Roz stepped up and shook Blake's hand too and got to bathe in those blue eyes one more time. *Wowzer.* That electric, effortless charisma—that was why Blake Burbage was a movie star.

Despite the courtesies and Blake's seeming candor, as she and Alden said goodbye and headed out, she had an uncomfortable sensation that they knew less than they did before they began.

Writer Sheryl—and Nicole, via Sebastian Esquivel—apparently had production deals with Wayne Vandershell. But Sebastian wasn't thrilled with the dead guy, and Blake Burbage seemed to think Wayne had been leading him on.

Could the cool Blake Burbage have killed Wayne Vandershell?

chapter
thirteen

ALDEN OPENED the passenger door for Roz, then walked around and slipped into the low seat and cranked up the Miata. He left the roof up, sensitive to Roz's desire to keep her hair tamed, even though it was pinned up in an adorable twist that made him want to undo it and run his fingers through it. Wasn't that half the fun in putting it up in the first place?

She was awfully quiet as the gate opened.

"You OK with what just transpired?" he asked as he rolled through and headed south on the beach road.

"What? Sorry, I was just thinking ... and yes. You were clear. We report the truth. And we're not out to make anyone's life miserable. Unless he killed the guy."

Alden snorted. "So I'm not the only one who had that thought."

"I mean, he sounded more annoyed than angry, but he is a good actor."

"Very good."

"And he had opportunity—he could have confronted Wayne on Saturday," Roz went on. "No idea about him tampering with the vape pen, though. It does seem like two crimes. Tampering seems cold and deliberate, but anyone who spent time with him could've found a way to do that. The thing is, they had no guarantee the vape pen would kill him. Harm him, certainly. But kill him? Was it mischievous? Malicious? While hitting him seems like an act of anger."

"The vape pen was certainly dangerous. Maybe the saboteur was ticked off that their battery hadn't exploded yet and wanted to make sure of the thing," Alden suggested.

"What an indirect way to kill someone. It's America. They could've just shot him."

Alden barked out a surprised laugh as he paused at a red light. "Sadly true, but you have a point. Even if it was all just a sinister prank gone horribly wrong, it's a good story, what with all the broken dreams and celebrity connections."

"And there's more, don't you think? I think Wayne was in the business of building up people's dreams, but I don't know if he ever intended to make any of them come true."

"It does seem that way," Alden agreed, pressing forward as the light changed. "Though Enolia seemed to like him. Maybe Mae did, too. Sheryl more than liked him. And who knows about Nicole Esquivel?"

"All of them women," Roz noted wryly. "But have they told us everything?"

"They've told us very little," he admitted. "One thing we know for sure is that he hadn't delivered on any of his promises. Or maybe I should say implied promises, based on what Blake said. How many of his acquaintances wanted him dead?" They were getting into the more commercial area of hotels and restaurants and tourist emporiums. "Need anything before we head to the movie studio? Coffee? Hamburger? Novelty beach towel?"

She snickered. "Thanks, but I'm good for now. Though

maybe we can hit the Milky Way sometime. I've been craving their butter pecan ice cream."

"Funny, I was just thinking we need to go back there."

She gave him a warm look, and he knew she was remembering that lovely day when he talked her into staying in Comet Cove.

"I should probably work off that Reuben sandwich first," she said.

"I can think of a few ways to do that." He shot her an impish grin.

"Ha!" He loved her flustered smile. "We have to *work* work," she told him, pulling her laptop from her bag. "I'm going to type up some of these notes while you get us to the studio."

"Which is where exactly? Other than near the airport."

"Oh, right." She picked up his phone where it was plugged into the car's upgraded electronics and started the navigation.

Alden let her work on her laptop as he wended south and eventually over the inlet bridge (how many times a week did he drive over that bridge?). He drove past the southside neighborhoods, the wildlife preserve and Vesper Lakes Golf Club.

The land started to open up a bit, with patches of scrub pine and palmettos between sprawling lots and industrial-looking businesses. The far south end of Comet Cove still had room for development, though maybe not for long.

What developers giveth, hurricanes taketh away, he mused. Though there was no sense in borrowing trouble.

As they slid past the small airport and its attendant hangars, more warehouses came into view. Some were kept well, but as they turned west down a poorly paved road, they found a less promising destination: a complex of hulking, weatherbeaten metal structures with an air of abandonment, surrounded by a six-foot-tall chain-link fence.

Alden pulled up outside a double gate, which stood open, padlock and chain dangling from one side. A small sign bore only the street address—no other labels, not *Vandershell Studios* or whatever it was supposed to be called. And no obvious movie set.

Roz had put away her laptop and stared through the windshield. "Doesn't look like much."

"And you want to get a picture."

"Yeah, since Kai couldn't make it. He's been ordered to the golf course."

"Again." Alden glanced at her. "Shall we?"

"Might as well. I'm guessing Sebastian is already in there since the gate is open."

"Why do I feel like I'm entering a scene in a horror movie?" He drove through anyway, tires crunching on gravel.

"I think you have movies on the brain."

"Can you blame me? I got to touch Blake's button compass!"

She laughed out loud. "Hey, look—that must be Sebastian."

As they moved up the drive, a large black SUV came into view, parked by one of the warehouses. And beyond, more structures with a hint of color.

"Could that be the street set he told me about?" she asked with enthusiasm.

"See, I'm not the only one with movies on the brain."

"Well, it's cool. Imagine if there really were a movie studio here."

"And even more starlets underfoot," he said.

"Not that you would mind. Speaking of, who was that Lexie person? Blake's girlfriend?"

He stopped the car next to the SUV, turned it off and turned to look at her. "Really? You don't know? It's Lexie Wintergarten. She won a supporting actress Oscar last year. And she's got to be twenty years younger than he is. He's a lucky guy. She's talented *and* beautiful."

"*Really*." Roz smirked at him. "And no, I had no idea."

"She's not as beautiful as you." He leaned in and gave her a tender, lingering kiss, and she sighed. "Ready?" he asked.

Roz blinked and smiled. "Yes."

He always liked hearing her say yes.

As they climbed out of the car, the SUV engine's rumble stopped and the driver's door opened. Sebastian Esquivel stepped out. Or, more accurately, down—the behemoth vehicle was twice the height of Alden's.

"I see you found it. Behold the Hollywood glamour," Sebastian said. He was a sturdy guy with dark hair wearing something that looked like a golfing outfit. Alden appreciated the sarcasm.

Roz spoke. "Sebastian, this is Alden Knox. He's working with me on the story."

"Nice to meet you," Alden said. They shook hands, and Sebastian gave him a knowing look. So he'd seen the kiss. Alden didn't care. If Alden had his way, he and Roz would be making out. Or holding hands and gamboling up and down the beach.

Maybe later. He did have *some* work ethic.

"Have you started work inside these buildings?" Roz asked while digging her camera out of her bag.

"Work, yes, though it might not be obvious to the eye," Sebastian said as they walked with him down the gravel road. He gestured to one of the four warehouses; there were two on each side of the road. "My crew did a little work on this one to make it structurally sound and started framing out a control booth and adding wiring, but the money I'd budgeted for this phase ran out pretty quick with Wayne not pitching in. Not much to see."

The closest warehouse looked a little better than the others, but Alden never would've guessed it had any work done.

"How did funding work, exactly?" Roz asked, snapping photos.

"We had a contract and an escrow account we were both supposed to contribute to," Sebastian replied. "Only he provided the lawyer who was supposed to oversee it, and I think the guy wasn't totally honest. Because Wayne hadn't invested his share by the time he died, even though we'd signed the agreement. I blame myself for taking him at his word."

"What happens now that he's dead?" Alden asked.

"That's a good question. I need to ask my lawyer to look at the agreement," Sebastian said. "I know I should've paid more attention, but I never foresaw any of this happening—Wayne flaking on me and then him dying."

They walked on for a minute toward the odd structures before Roz asked, "Is that the movie street you told me about? If the warehouse isn't interesting, maybe we could see the set."

"'Set' is a strong word. I'll show you what we've got. It's not much." The builder led them forward. As they rounded the curve, more of the colorful structures came into view.

They were—houses. Only something wasn't quite right about them. They were cute—a cottage with white siding, a two-story brick affair, a yellow stucco bungalow, all with colorful trim—set close together on a paved road. They looked plucked from an idyllic suburban neighborhood, complete with green lawns (fake grass, Alden thought), pretty landscaping, a sidewalk and mailboxes. But the paved "street" stopped several feet beyond them on either side. And a fourth "house" stood half-built, a fraction of facade surrounded by wood framing, with nothing behind it at all.

It became clear as they got closer that the three perfect houses were also illusions, fancy fronts with convincing side walls and partial roofs, if you didn't look at them from too much of an angle. With no dressing on the windows, it was easy to peer inside and see that the empty indoor spaces stopped a few feet beyond the front walls.

Sebastian halted in the middle of the paved street. "We had plans to build them out, make real buildings with some interior locations as well as exteriors. Add to the street, maybe make a town square."

"Like a real backlot," Alden said. "That's ambitious."

Sebastian caught Alden's skeptical tone. "Like I told Roz, movies aren't my business. I trusted Wayne. I have no idea if this would've worked. If filmmakers would come here."

Roz seemed fascinated. "These look great, even if you didn't finish them. We have a lot of beautiful locations in the area, too. I could totally see this working. I mean, if it was ever completed. But I'm not in the biz either."

"There you go," Sebastian said. "It's easy to forget the practicalities. I'm not a creative type, but the idea caught my imagination. Maybe I got in too deep."

"Mind if I walk around to take some pictures?" she asked.

"Go ahead." Sebastian waved a hand at the mini street.

So she did, snapping Sebastian talking in front of the structures, getting a few shots from the back to show the illusion. Finally, she asked, "Are there any other sets or locations?"

"This property goes all the way to the lagoon, but we

haven't done much with it yet. There's a small lake and a wooded area. Both would be great for filming, or so I was told." Sebastian seemed resigned to his "studio" becoming a ghost town.

Yet Alden could see how he'd been enticed to build this. He, too, could imagine movies shooting here. "We'd love to see the rest."

"It would involve hiking through the scrub," Sebastian answered. "I'd rather we didn't."

"Oh, well." Roz stuffed her camera back in her bag. "Too bad we don't have a drone. We could shoot it from above."

Sebastian's face lit up. "I can do you one better. Want to fly over it?"

chapter
fourteen

"THIS DAY HAS TAKEN A TURN." Roz couldn't hide her excitement as Alden drove them toward Comet Cove Airport, following Sebastian's SUV. They were back on the paved road, and Sebastian had locked up the nascent movie studio.

"Did you know he was a pilot?" Alden asked.

"I had no idea, but how could we turn down his offer?"

"Flying over the site is not strictly necessary for the story, but I suppose it'll be good photos."

Roz looked over at him, sensing something else in his tone. "Are you nervous?"

Alden shrugged, focusing on the road. "I'm more comfortable in boats than small airplanes."

"Even after—you know?" She flashed back on an unfortunate boat ride during the pursuit of their last big story.

He humphed. "Yes. Boats don't fall out of the sky."

"Oh, stop it. You traveled all over the world for the *National Eye*. Surely some small planes were involved."

"They were. I'll be fine." But he still sounded funny.

"What happened? Something happened, didn't it?"

Alden sighed. "My father's a private pilot. He took my

brother and I up sometimes when we were kids. He was trying to land in a storm and—well, we had a hard landing short of the runway."

A shiver ran through Roz. She could've lost Alden before she even met him. "How hard of a landing?"

He lifted one shoulder, not taking his eyes off the road. "A wing broke off. But we were OK."

"A *wing broke off*? What in the actual— How have you not told me this before?"

"It never came up."

And the timing of his story wasn't great, given they were about to fly in Sebastian's plane, but she *did* ask. She wasn't nervous, though. She looked forward to the flight. She'd never flown in a small plane.

"Do you want to stay behind?" she asked him.

"Hell, no. I'm OK with flying. As you pointed out, I've flown a lot. I just always take a moment to think about my mortality before I get on a flight, and I try to eat dessert first. Preferably with a good whiskey."

She wasn't sure if he was joking. "OK, if you're sure. I think it's kind of an adventure."

"I never thought you'd be a secret adventure girl."

"Maybe you've given me a taste for danger."

"Ha," he said. "I haven't even gotten started. Here we are."

The entrance to the airport bore a vertical rack of signs touting tourist flights, flying lessons, helicopter rides, biplane rides, an aerial sign-towing company, generically named aviation firms, and the Comet Cove Sheriff's Department Aviation Unit. Which Roz happened to know supported only visiting aircraft from the county or the state police, since their town was way too small to afford any flying machine bigger than a drone.

They followed Sebastian to a parking lot behind one of the hangars and exited their vehicles. Alden threw his jacket into the Miata, and Roz left her bag behind, taking only her camera. She didn't want any carry-on luggage.

She trailed the guys through a small door, past an enclosed office and into a cavernous space with a tall, gently peaked ceiling.

The big doors were open, facing the runway. Two planes sat on the shiny concrete floor—one red and white, the other a bright yellow biplane with a tool-covered cart sitting next to it.

"Whoa," said Alden, who had an eye for cars. Maybe he liked good-looking aircraft, too.

Roz personally hoped Sebastian's plane was the red-and-white one. It looked more modern and less likely to force her to wing-walk. She was relieved when he walked toward it.

Then a head popped up from the cockpit of the biplane. "Seb! You going out?" called a man with tousled blond hair and a tan and weathered face.

"Jesus, Chuck, you startled me," Sebastian exclaimed.

Chuck climbed out and hopped to the floor in his stained tan mechanic's jumpsuit, wearing a wily smile. "Just thought I'd work in some time on my baby between jobs. Hey, Alden."

Roz looked at Alden in surprise.

"Chuck, good to see you in your natural environment."

"Haven't seen you much around the Rusty Rocket lately," Chuck said.

"I've been busy," Alden replied. "Working a lot."

"I know how that is." Chuck looked toward her expectantly.

Sebastian introduced Roz. "Chuck does a lot of maintenance work for people around here, including my Cessna." He turned to the mechanic. "Can you give me a hand?"

"Sure." Chuck helped Sebastian use a tow bar to pull the Cessna out of the hangar, then looked at his watch. "I've got an appointment down the alley. Have fun." A moment later, he strolled away with a bag of tools over his shoulder.

Sebastian told the reporters, "I need to run my checklist. There's a restroom back by the office, and there's a vending machine in there if you want anything."

"There's your chance to eat dessert first," Roz murmured to Alden as Sebastian got started on preflight checks.

He snorted. "No, thanks. I'd rather have a nice dinner later with you."

"Or would you rather go to the Rusty Rocket?"

Alden smiled. "I had to do something to pass the time before I met you. It's a dive, but they have good bands."

"You'll have to take me sometime."

Alden and Roz each took advantage of the restroom, then Roz checked her camera to be sure she had a fresh battery and plenty of room on the memory cards.

It took Sebastian just over ten minutes to complete his checks, punctuated by a couple of reverberating sneezes, and then he invited them to climb aboard. No stairs were needed —the plane wasn't that big. Roz and Alden entered the door under the wing on the passenger side.

"I want to sit in the back so I can move from window to window," Roz said as she ducked into the second row, which had two seats. The plane had only four, and calling it cozy was generous.

"I love the front," Alden said with a touch of sarcasm as he settled in the seat next to their pilot, who handed them head-phones with a microphone attached so they could talk.

Sebastian touched buttons and switches while scanning a laminated checklist. "Make sure your harnesses are secure for takeoff. You might be able to move around later. Waist first, then click in the shoulder straps."

Alden was way ahead of him, door secured and already buckled in, and Roz buckled hers, too, after a minute of figuring out the system. Though she hoped to free herself later and shoot from both sides of the plane.

Her adrenaline jumped as Sebastian turned a key and the engine roared to life. After more checks, he called out on the radio. "Comet Cove traffic. November one seven niner Bay Rays, departing runway one-one southbound. Comet Cove traffic," he repeated.

Roz chuckled at the "Bay Rays." Hardcore baseball fan, indeed.

No one called back, and Sebastian took a good look around to make sure no one was leaving or landing before he lined up for takeoff. And then they were rolling down the runway with the sun behind them.

"You two all right?" Sebastian asked, his voice slightly distorted through the headset.

"All good," Roz said.

"Fine," Alden answered. Was he?

Roz reached forward and touched his shoulder, and he shot her a smile over his shoulder. He seemed fine. But she wondered if she should've bought him a chocolate bar anyway.

"Takeoff," Sebastian said.

They lifted off the ground, wobbling a bit, climbing. She could've sworn the engine hiccuped, and Alden sent their pilot a sharp look. But Sebastian's face betrayed no concern, so Roz decided not to worry either. He knew what he was doing.

The view quickly captured her attention as he banked the plane toward the south. "We'll look at the studio lot first, and then I'll show you all of Comet Cove if you're interested," Sebastian said.

"Awesome," Roz answered.

Sunset was still more than an hour away, but the aging daylight touched the sky with magic. Only a few wisps of cloud remained after the earlier rain, and they glowed with a pale amber light against a sky of softened blue.

The plane leveled, and Roz looked out and snapped photos of the land below where it abutted the Indian River Lagoon. She wasn't a hundred percent sure she was shooting the right thing, as there weren't a lot of buildings south of the airport, but then she saw the tiny facades of the fake street and zoomed in to snap several pictures.

Now that she knew she was looking in the right place, it was easy to find the lake Sebastian had mentioned. It was definitely woodsy around it. There was a lot of space and a lot of potential. She popped open her seat harness and moved to the other side to take more pictures.

"Got it?" came Sebastian's voice in her ear.

"Got it!" she said, and he changed direction, arcing north even as he gained altitude. The engine coughed again.

She and Alden exchanged a glance.

"Great view, isn't it?" Sebastian said. He sounded calm, but he looked at the dash with concern.

What was going on? The engine sounded rough. Was this normal?

Roz pushed down a bubble of worry and decided to trust his skills and take advantage of the opportunity. She took a few photos, but mostly she enjoyed the spectacle—Comet Cove, breathtakingly small from up here, like a toy village, vulnerable and beautiful with the inlet bisecting it. The ocean on one side seemed greener than the dusky blue of the lagoon on the other. The strip of sand marking the beach almost made a straight line; the shore of the river side undulated with curves and points. The red-and-white stripes of the lighthouse stood out, and greenery softened the hard lines of neighborhoods.

She moved to the seat behind Alden, then again to the one behind Sebastian, taking photos from as many angles as she could. As she snapped, the engine sputtered ...

"Um," Alden said.

... and then it died.

And time compressed.

Sebastian muttered a curse under his breath. "Harness on," he snapped as he worked the controls.

Inwardly, Roz cursed, too. She dropped back into the seat behind him and wrangled herself into the belts as Sebastian turned in a hard arc.

Before she even realized she'd broken out in a cold sweat, Sebastian was calling on the radio, "Mayday, Mayday, Mayday. November one seven niner Bravo Romeo. We've lost the engine. Three people on board. Heading back toward Comet Cove airfield."

We've lost the engine?

He'd dropped the cutesy coda to the tail number, a sure sign that fun time was over.

"There's no control tower at the airport, is there?" Roz asked.

"No," Alden said grimly.

"I'm alerting emergency services and any aircraft in the area." Sebastian's voice was shockingly cool as he addressed them. "We're going to try to reach the runway."

"Try?" Roz squeaked.

"I can't restart the engine," the pilot said. "I don't think we're going to make it."

chapter
fifteen

THIS FELT LIKE A MOVIE. A movie Alden really didn't want to be in.

Their plane plummeted. Or glided with a vengeance. However he wrote it in his head, the Cessna descended at an alarming rate. *We aren't high enough*, he thought.

Sebastian confirmed his fears.

"Mayday, Mayday, Mayday. November one seven niner Bravo Romeo. We've lost the engine. Can't make the strip. We're going to ditch in the river west of Comet Cove." Sebastian's delivery was crisp as he called out on the radio, adding their coordinates and direction.

Alden turned his head and caught Roz's eye, reached a hand back to her. She grabbed it.

He wasn't ready to lose Roz.

"Hold on to your harness," Sebastian ordered, terse and urgent, and Alden reluctantly released Roz's hand and complied, grabbing the vertical belts on his restraints. "Going flaps full," the pilot said in the radio callout voice again. Then to them: "I've got to go in as slow as I can. Don't worry. Ninety percent of water landings are nonfatal."

"Fantastic," Alden muttered, and Roz emitted one of those brief, hysterical giggles that happen when everything is going to hell.

He hoped they could laugh about this later.

What happened to the engine? How deep was the water here? Would they make it?

"Roz, grab the life jackets under your seat and give one to Alden," Sebastian said. "Put them around your necks."

Alden glanced back as she searched. "They're right there. Yellow and flat," he told her.

"Oh, OK." She grabbed them, the type he'd seen demonstrated on airline flights countless times. "I was thinking of those fat life jackets. Not the inflatable ones." She handed one to Alden and put another around her neck.

"Do you want one, Sebastian?" she called.

"Busy right now," he growled in the headset.

The surface of the lagoon still rushed toward them, but the rate of approach slowed slightly. The flaps doing their work, Alden thought. He had a dim sense of the distant shorelines on either side as a blur in his peripheral vision.

Sebastian, to his astonishment, turned the lever on his door and cracked it open. "Crack open your door if you can."

Alden did as he was told, the open doors adding a new rattle to the rushing noise of their descent. Alden's mind worked over Sebastian's reasoning. The plane was going to crash-land in the water. He supposed it was like a car that drives into a lake. When a car goes under, water pressure can keep the occupants from opening the doors. So they were opening them in advance. That had to be it.

Also, this is madness.

The water was so close now. The plane's angle tilted up as

Sebastian flared the wings a bit, then leveled them, and the Cessna leveled too.

With a bone-shaking shudder, the plane half skimmed, half plowed into the water.

Water felt soft when you swam around in it. But when you slammed into it at highway speeds, it felt more like half-dry concrete.

The force of impact threw Alden forward against the belts, then backward as the plane's nose tipped up. There were a couple of breathtaking moments when he wondered if it would keep going and somersault forward, or flip to its back on the rebound. But to his relief, when the plane rocked back, it stayed right side up as it settled in the water.

Which rushed in the open doors, swarming around his feet.

The headrest, the harness—both had kept him from launching. But now they had a deluge to contend with.

He took a second to look back. Roz seemed shaken but OK. She gave him a thumbs-up. In her other hand, she still carried her camera, the strap wrapped tightly around her wrist. Fear flashed in her eyes as she took in the water swirling around their legs.

First thought: *She's alive. We're alive!*

Second thought: *I should've recorded this on my phone for the paper.*

Third: *This water isn't good, is it?*

"We have to get out." Sebastian, already free of his harness, spoke in fast, clipped tones as he grabbed a GoPro camera off its overhead mount and stuffed it and his tablet computer into a small bag. "The water's pretty shallow here, but I'm not exactly sure how deep. We don't want to be in here if the plane sinks." Alden got out of his restraint fast, too—past experience

—and reached back to help Roz, but she managed to release hers a second later without his help. The rising water was a strong motivator.

He yanked off his headset and started pushing on his door. It resisted.

Roz, who'd also shed her headset, tried to help Sebastian fully open the port-side door while keeping her camera above the water.

"What are you doing with that stupid camera?" said Alden, who could now about wedge himself through the door.

"It's practically brand new! I don't want to lose it to the river."

"Just get out!" Sebastian said, and he plunged through the door and into the river proper.

"Please!" Alden added.

She squeezed through the door after their pilot, and then she was out the other side, so Alden half fell out his, stumbling in the water.

Stumbling. *Yes!* His feet touched the silty floor of the Indian River Lagoon. The cool water sloshed around his chest. At least they weren't in over their heads, and there wasn't a current to speak of. He didn't even have to inflate his life vest.

Not yet.

"Roz?" he called out.

"Over here with Sebastian!"

Alden took a few steps and looked around, getting his bearings. Roz and Sebastian were angling east in the river, away from the plane, Roz still with her camera hand in the air. He laughed to himself. That was so Roz.

Then again, maybe he could save his phone. He pulled it out of his pants pocket and held it higher as he sloshed away from the Cessna.

The plane faced south, and he was pretty sure the nose was lower than it was a moment ago. Comet Cove and the airfield, wherever it was, were to his left, the direction Roz and Sebastian were moving.

He made a wide, awkward circle around the nose of the Cessna, then waded through the chest-high water toward the other two, sluggish and heavy in his drenched clothes. He guessed the shore was less than a mile away.

The water depth decreased by a few inches, hitting him just above the waist as he neared Roz and Sebastian. The bedraggled pair had stopped and turned to face the plane. Roz snapped pictures of the wreck. Sebastian was on the phone, probably calling emergency services.

Alden wanted to touch Roz, maybe out of an urgent need to assure himself she was really there. That they really were OK. But she was busy. There'd be time later.

He looked back at their ride. The nose had tipped forward now and was mostly submerged—they were lucky to get out before it was inundated. The tail stuck up and looked distressed, but it was hard to make out all the damage he knew was there.

There was certainly invisible damage that might explain why they were standing in the middle of the river in their clothes. Crash investigators would have to find out why the engine died. Alden wanted to know, too.

Someone killed Wayne. And now Sebastian had almost died, along with his two hapless passengers.

If this was a coincidence, it was a mighty unnerving one.

All three of them just stood there in the river as the plane settled. Roz took her photos, and Sebastian, holding his bag above the water, made another phone call—to his wife, judging by his soothing tones and the screeches on the other end of the line.

Alden checked his phone. To his relief, it had also survived. He shot John a quick text:

> Roz and I OK after Cessna 172 crash in river. Engine died suddenly, approx ten minutes after takeoff from Comet Cove airport. Pilot Sebastian Esquivel also OK. No other passengers. Emergency services contacted. More later.

There you go. John could make a story out of that. Alden turned on the camera app and shot several seconds of video of the plane and his fellow survivors, along with a few photos, which he texted to John.

Who wrote back with a torrent of words that included, "When were you going to tell me you were getting on a plane with your subject?"

Yeah, maybe they should've thought that through. Alden would talk to him later. In the meantime, he held his phone above the water instead of returning it to his pocket. No sense in pushing his luck. Roz, seeing him, mouthed a silent curse, pulled her phone from an underwater pocket and peered at it. Then she smiled.

Hooray for modern technology.

Now that they'd paused in documenting the crash, Alden looked at Sebastian, who'd ended his call. "Nice landing."

"Thank you." A corner of Sebastian's mouth turned down. "Sorry to put you through that."

"I'm sorry you lost your plane," Alden replied. "What do you think happened?"

"I damn well better find out." Sebastian sneezed. "The engine died, obviously. I don't know why. Oil pressure seemed OK. A blocked valve? I don't know. I did all the checks. It almost sounded like—nah, it couldn't be. I checked the fuel, too."

"You think it was the fuel? Water in it, maybe?"

Sebastian threw an intense look at Alden. "You fly?"

"My dad had a small plane."

"Well, I don't know. I just don't know. It looked OK when I sumped it ..." Sebastian hesitated, as if he were thinking it over. "We're going to have to get the carcass back to shore, and then the NTSB is going to want to take a look. What a royal pain in the potato."

Alden almost smiled. "I want to know what happened, too."

"Of course," the builder replied.

"Should we start walking back?" Alden hoped there weren't holes deeper than the four feet of water they were currently in. A walk wasn't going to be pleasant, and he wasn't sure where they were. He looked more closely at the shore. Was that a marina? Not big enough to be Star Harbor, and they weren't looking at the inlet. Southside Wharf, then.

A blinking light caught his eye. A blinking blue light attached to the shape of a boat, which was getting bigger.

Roz was looking now, too. "I think it's Duke."

Alden groaned.

"Duke?" Sebastian asked.

"Deputy Duke. Duke Dawson." Alden added wryly, "Roz's boyfriend."

"He is *not*!" she exclaimed. "Alden's teasing me. We had a few dates in high school, that's all."

Sebastian actually laughed. "Well, I'm glad that's all,

because you two looked pretty friendly back there at the movie studio."

Roz gave Alden a cross look, and he laughed, too.

The happy thought came again: *We're alive!*

And now damnable Deputy Duke was going to *rescue* them. Didn't Comet Cove have other police officers? Alden was kind of fuzzy on how many. Not his beat. It was a small department, that much he knew. But Duke seemed to have an instinct for being wherever Roz was.

At least they wouldn't have to wade all the way home.

"That's lucky," Roz was saying. "I wasn't looking forward to slogging to shore."

"We could have been luckier," Alden groused. A shiver ran through him as he tried to ignore the seaweedy smell of the chilly brine. "Next time I'm having dessert first."

DUKE'S FACE said it all as he gave them their ride to shore. Specifically: You two are a wreck, you smell like a bait bucket, and how do you keep ending up like this?

Or maybe that was the voice in Alden's head. He was fine, though they were checked out by an ambulance crew, wrapped in blankets and given bad coffee—after he and Roz shared a very long hug. Deputy Byrd briefly interviewed them as Duke dealt with Sebastian and arrangements for the plane.

It had been an insanely long day, and Alden needed a shower and a meal and to hold Roz. He'd almost lost her. They'd almost lost each other.

Alden called Toby, who usually drove for Rideeo, for a lift to the airport so they could pick up his car. Then Roz called John and filled him in while Alden drove them back to her house—the house she grew up in. It had a mid-century vibe Roz was accenting with retro furnishings and lamps.

He liked the house. Mostly he liked being in her space. He kept a few things there—basics, some clothes. He'd love to move in, but he didn't think Roz was ready for that. Small steps.

He laid out the contents of his wallet on a towel on her dining table to dry out. They each took a shower, then ate a pizza from Pluto's and talked about what happened. He poured them a couple of glasses of nice California cabernet— he'd stocked Roz's kitchen with some good bottles. By the time they curled up on the couch in soft white robes he'd bought from Lunaria Lodge in a sentimental moment, he felt almost human.

"I feel like we should be working on a story," he told her, one arm around her as she snuggled into him and flipped through channels on the modest TV, settling on classic movies. She knew they were his comfort watch, and she seemed to like them, too.

"You mean a story about the crash?" Roz put down the remote and picked up her glass of wine. "We should be good for now. John posted something short and sweet, based on what we told him, and I sent him a few more photos when you were in the shower. But he knows we'll have more later."

Alden eyed Humphrey Bogart negotiating with Sydney Greenstreet and harrumphed. "We'd better have more. We need to find out what caused that crash."

"I think you mean *who* caused that crash." She sipped her wine.

"We shouldn't jump to conclusions, but that's exactly what I mean," Alden said. "I can't believe that engine failure was a coincidence. Sebastian was Wayne's partner. Wayne is dead. So how would killing Sebastian benefit anyone?"

"Again, *who* would it benefit? With Wayne, it seems like somebody didn't like him, at the very least. Maybe somebody gained satisfaction by seeing him dead. But Sebastian?"

"His wife? It's always the wife."

"Or the husband," Roz said dryly. "I don't know. That's a

grim thought. But it makes a weird kind of sense." Roz set her wine on the rectangular wooden coffee table and shifted so she could look up at him. She was so deliciously warm. He told his body to behave itself as she went on. "Nicole seemed so nice. Though she was annoyed with Sebastian Saturday when he didn't show up on time to take the kids."

"Do you think she had a grudge against Wayne, too?"

"She had the opportunity to confront him Saturday if she wanted to, when she left the kids in the bathroom. But if you're talking motive for murder, I don't know."

"We just don't know enough," Alden said. "I think you need to talk to her. And we need to get more out of Enolia about Wayne."

"Maybe through Craig, her assistant."

"Right. Good idea. I could reach out to him directly, tell him I need some basic facts about her book catalog and I don't want to bug her about it."

"You don't have to lie," Roz told him.

"You're right. I'll just tell him I need to ask him a few questions, OK?"

"OK." She smiled, lifted her face, and accepted his quick kiss. Before he could get any ideas, she continued, "I also want to get a look at that agreement between Wayne Vandershell and Sebastian Esquivel that Sebastian seemed so vague about. He said he didn't know what the terms were if one of them died. I want to know."

"Excellent idea. You'll have to ask him. Do you think he'll let you see it?"

"I suppose it depends on if he's hiding something," she said. "If he says no, that's one way we'll know that he is. I mean, I'd expect most people to be circumspect about their business dealings, but he already told us a lot, and he didn't seem like a detail guy when it came to the legal stuff. I'm betting he'll let me see the contract."

Alden put down his wine and kissed her again, more slowly this time. He fingered the lapel of her robe as her eyes grew dreamy. "He'll say yes to you."

And then she yawned.

And he yawned. "Argh. Does this mean we should sleep?"

"We should," she said impishly. "But we don't have to."

"Oh?" He raised an eyebrow hopefully and pitched his voice low. "What would you like to do?"

"I think we should comb the Internet and streaming services and find those movies Wayne made. They might tell us more about him."

Alden groaned. As she giggled, he pushed her gently off him and stood. "I'll get my laptop."

ALDEN HAD TOLD Roz he'd looked for Wayne Vandershell's movies online, and she believed him. But she also believed that working together, they could find those titles.

She was wrong.

They searched all the streaming services they could think of, including obscure artsy ones. No movies.

They searched the Web for him again. Besides the school-days tidbits they'd unearthed earlier, they found a six-year-old speeding ticket in California and no outstanding charges. There were a couple of old addresses—apartments, it looked like.

The more recent stuff was scant but all film-related. They had his profile on the most popular movie database site and a few similar profiles elsewhere. There was a press release focused on Wayne that had gone around for one of his movies, noting it had been selected for three major film festivals—but didn't mention which ones.

"So it's a press release. Anyone can write a press release," Roz said, enjoying her cozy spot next to Alden on the couch as he drove the laptop. "Who sent it out?"

Alden looked for the fine print on a few of the places where it appeared until he found the common thread. "It's one of those online-only publicity outfits."

"Is it a scam?"

"I've seen it before. It's not a scam in the sense that they do the work they're hired to do. But I don't think they verify what they send out. You hire them, and they send the release everywhere. And some 'news' sites just publish whatever releases come down the pipe for clicks and SEO, sometimes automatically. It's rinse and repeat, and if you're lucky, somebody quotes it and the news spreads further."

"And whoever picks it up gives it legitimacy whether it's valid or not," Roz said. "It's like online rumors that get so much air through repetition that everyone starts to think they're true. What about the other people listed as filmmakers with him?"

Alden clicked through the slim list of credits on Wayne's producer projects. Every one of the names was linked to another of Wayne's movies. The movies they couldn't find. From name to name, it was like a recursive loop—they all worked on one another's projects, but quick Web searches didn't pull up any of the others' films either.

"Were these guys even real?" Alden navigated back to Wayne's profile. "I'm going to try to contact one of them. This Reynold Casper guy. See what I can get." He searched around until he found an email address, then hammered out a message. "Sent."

"Good luck," Roz said fondly. She enjoyed it when Alden got going.

A few minutes later, his laptop dinged. "Reynold Casper wrote me back."

"Already? What does he say?"

"He says that the short films aren't available right now due to sensitive negotiations, but he's available for production work anytime."

"What negotiations?" Roz didn't like how vague that sounded.

"I'll ask him, and I'll also see if one of these other guys responds." He sent more emails to Reynold Casper and two of his friends. A few minutes passed as they watched Humphrey Bogart handle the Fat Man and the femme fatale. Alden also googled Reynold Casper, who, if his social media reflected reality, worked as a guide on Disneyland's Jungle Cruise.

Alden's email program dinged again. "Ha. One of Reynold's friends says the short films aren't available right now because they're tied up in negotiations. And Reynold wrote back to say he can't give more details. I call BS. All of these supposed films can't be tied up in 'negotiations.'"

"That's certainly vague."

"Wayne's credit for *Fastest Spin Wins* is legit," Alden said. "That's the one my friend Porter worked on."

"One legit project," Roz observed. "A bunch not so legit, I'm guessing. I'm confident we would've found at least one of these somewhere if they were real. Or Wayne would've embedded a short film on his website or something. But his site is pretty sketchy, too."

"Right. He just links to the credits on the movie database

and talks vaguely about all the great work he has in development."

"I can't say I'm surprised at this point, but I think Wayne has been a very bad boy," Roz said, "and not in a good way."

"But to what end? He'd dangled deals in front of writers, in front of Sebastian Esquivel, in front of Blake Burbage even. Did he come through for anyone? What was his end game?"

"What does anyone want in the end?" she mused. "Fame? Credit?"

"Money," they said at the same time.

Roz was skeptical. "Was he trying to get money out of the writers?"

Alden snorted. "Talk about barking up the wrong tree."

"At least where most writers are concerned." She thought for a second. "But if Wayne targeted them for their money, not their talent ... We need to talk to Sheryl again, too."

"Enolia has the talent."

"And gobs of money," Roz added.

"Could Sebastian have been in on whatever the scheme was?"

"I doubt it. He didn't seem very taken with Wayne."

"Wayne was courting Blake, too, who's rich enough," Alden said. "Though Blake didn't mention any money changing hands. I need to ask him about that."

Roz sat up. "Now that you mention Blake ..."

"Yeah?"

"He's a total airplane geek. He has all that flying memorabilia. He has a plane at Comet Cove airport. Do you think he knows something about Sebastian's plane?"

Alden set his laptop on the coffee table and looked at her. "Or worse? Do you think Blake would try to kill Sebastian? Why? Something to do with the movie studio?"

Roz shrugged. "That I don't know. But he might know something about what went on at the airport. It's a small place. He might even know Sebastian. We should see what Blake knows."

"First let me see if I can get any technical information about the crash before it's official. I have an idea of how to go about that. You can ping Sebastian about the contract."

"Ugh. We have a long day tomorrow." Roz fell back and leaned against him, and he slipped an arm around her shoulders.

"That's OK. I'm just glad we *have* a tomorrow. There was a minute today—"

"I know. I'm glad too." Roz paused. "And I'm mad. Mad at whoever sabotaged that plane, assuming it wasn't an accident. Which it might be."

"Where would the fun be in that?" he joked.

She quirked her mouth at him. "I would've had plenty of fun not crashing in the river, thanks. Now we're both going to be nervous before we fly."

"Don't worry, sweetheart." Alden kissed her head. "I'll make sure I have chocolate and good whiskey on hand."

And he pulled her closer and pressed his mouth to hers, sweet and hot.

Better than chocolate *or* whiskey.

seventeen

ROZ HAD to show her face at the office Tuesday morning and check in with the reporters to make sure everyone was on track. Alden suggested they might as well face John's dressing-down now. So she put on nice black pants with a cute wide belt, a white tank, a cropped black denim jacket and short boots with a low heel, preparing for battle.

Alden drove them to the *Courier-Beacon* office downtown. Her car was still parked outside. She'd need it. They expected to be on different tracks again today.

Oh, who was she kidding? She had no idea what track she'd be on today. That was one reason she loved this job.

What she didn't love was John's scolding. Why were they gallivanting about in an airplane? Why didn't they ask him before they went? And why didn't they get Hai to go along? He seemed to forget Hai was off pursuing golf pros.

On the other hand, John was super excited about all the clicks, partly because Webb Howard, their absentee publisher, had sent him a Way To Go email this morning.

They finally escaped his glass office and ran into Bruce,

who'd just topped off his Star Trek mug at the coffee station. "That looked like it hurt," he said with a smirk.

"He's not the only one who can inflict pain around here," Roz told him.

Bruce blanched. "Geez, touchy." But he was smiling as he scampered off to his desk.

They also ran into Hai, who'd stopped by to pick up a package. "I hear John was upset you didn't ask me to go along on the flight."

"A little," Alden replied. "Sorry about that."

"I really appreciate your not asking me. You two are cursed." The photographer's mouth twitched with humor. "I'm off to hunt down nudists with Janice." And he was off, leaving only Bruce typing away with his headphones on.

"So glad we're such a source of amusement for the staff," Roz muttered as she headed toward her corner.

"We're helping morale," Alden said wryly, dropping into the chair next to her desk. He looked delicious in dark jeans and a white button-up shirt, sleeves rolled up. He swam regularly at the gym. Roz went with him sometimes but did more looking than exercising.

"Shall we go over the trouble we're getting into today?" he asked, his eyes sparkling. He probably caught her looking.

"That's the problem. We don't know what the trouble is until we're in the middle of it. I've already sent Sebastian a request for the contract he had with Wayne. Hang on." Roz opened her laptop and checked her email. There was an email from Sebastian ... *yes*! "I almost can't believe it. He sent it to me. That's what I'll be working on. And I suppose I can't avoid some editing. I'm also hoping Sheryl drops by, but if she doesn't, I'm going to track her down."

"I'm going to the airport," Alden said. "I intend to find out more about our doomed plane."

"You have something in mind?"

"I do."

"Will you have time to press Enolia for more info about Wayne?"

"We talked about contacting Craig first," he said. "I can do that. Let's touch base later."

"Definitely stay in touch," Roz said. "I don't like the way this is going, and I don't want to worry about you."

He briefly caressed her shoulder as he stood, and the touch settled her.

"I'll be fine," he said. "I'm more worried about deadline."

"As you should be," she joked as she watched him leave. But she did worry about him. There was somebody scary out there doing bad things. And the more they learned, the more they put themselves in harm's way.

ALDEN SHOOK off the cold prickle that ran up his spine as he parked behind Sebastian Esquivel's hangar at the Comet Cove Airport.

It's OK. You're not getting on a plane today. No matter who asks.

He wondered idly if he needed therapy—not for the first time—as he locked up the Miata, opened the unlocked back door of the hangar and wandered in.

It was half empty. Chuck's biplane stood there. But Sebastian's Cessna 172 didn't. So where was it?

"Hello?" he called out. "Chuck?"

"Alden Knox," came a voice from behind him, and he

whirled, his heart hammering. He let out a breath when he saw it was Chuck in his jumpsuit.

"Damn it, Chuck, you scared me half to death."

"That's two days in a row you got a good scare, then," Chuck said with a rough chuckle. "Though yesterday you were scared almost *all the way* to death."

"Don't remind me. Do you know what happened to the plane?"

"After the crash? They brought down a construction barge from up the river and used a crane to pick it up just after sunrise. Dropped it on a truck at the airport's dock. Then a couple of NTSB people came and looked it over, and off it went."

"Already?" Alden checked his adventure watch. "Ten thirty? I wanted to get a look at it. Maybe talk to the investigators."

"They work pretty fast." Chuck's eyes twinkled.

Alden raised an eyebrow. "What do you know? Were you there?"

"Damn right I was there. I maintained that plane. There's no way the engine just died on me. I wanted to see what they did when they got it ashore."

Alden looked around, making sure they were alone. "Tell me how it went down."

Chuck wandered out to him, past him, toward the big open doors of the hangar, and Alden followed. There were hangars on either side of this one, running down the length of the small airport. The tarmac spread out before them, wide open, the runway stretching toward the water.

A small plane—a Piper Cherokee, he thought—filled the air with its drone as it accelerated down the runway, lifting as it passed in front of them, the pitch of the engine dipping in that satisfying Doppler-effect shift as it soared out over the lagoon.

"Flying lesson," Chuck said. "It takes some guts to do that the day after a crash."

They stood there, watching the plane get smaller and smaller, birdsong replacing the growl of the engine as the Piper flew away. Small white clouds hung around in the blue, still waking up, waiting to fluff and puff and rain on someone.

"You're killing me, Chuck. What did you see?" Alden was a pretty patient guy, usually. Patience worked for some sources. But he knew Chuck. And Alden had almost died yesterday. He had to know.

"They did a thorough inspection. I offered to help. Mostly they said no, but I made myself invaluable, and I was right there when they sampled the fuel."

Alden swallowed. "What about the fuel?"

"Contaminated. I have no doubt. I could smell the jet fuel."

"Jet fuel? But the Cessna uses avgas."

"Exactly."

"So it was an honest mistake? Sebastian put the wrong fuel in?"

"Absolutely not," Chuck said. "There are avgas pumps here —that's what most of the pilots use. That's what Sebastian uses. The jet fuel truck comes regularly, but Sebastian would never use it to fuel up. Somebody added just enough to kill the engine, little enough that the plane was able to get in the air. Was it running rough?"

"Yeah. And then it just croaked." A dim memory surfaced in Alden's mind. "I thought avgas had a particular color?"

"You're right. Sebastian should've seen the blue color when he sumped it during checks. But if there wasn't a lot of jet fuel in it, he might not've noticed. It still would've killed the engine. But I don't get why he didn't smell it." Chuck kicked at a pebble. "Makes me wonder if he knew all along. I know that's crazy, though. Sebastian loved that plane. And I don't think he'd invite passengers along on a kamikaze flight."

"That's a horrible thought. Thanks."

Chuck laughed at Alden's sarcasm. Then his face grew more serious. "I don't think that was it. He didn't notice, for whatever reason."

"He might've been in a hurry to get us in the air. Wait—he was sneezing yesterday."

"Oh, yeah!" Chuck brightened. "He's been kvetching about allergies for weeks."

"So maybe he couldn't smell it." Alden gave Chuck an intent look. "And you didn't notice anyone messing with the plane?"

"Chill, man. I'm here a lot, but we're pretty relaxed about the hangar. When people are around, it's open. When I go home for the day, I lock it up."

"So who got in here to contaminate the fuel?"

"That I don't know. But I've already ordered security cameras."

"Better late than never," Alden said dryly. "Hey, do you know Blake Burbage?"

"Are you asking as a friend or as a reporter?"

"Just answer the question. I'll owe you a beer."

"To think I'm so easily bought." Chuck smiled. "Off the record? Of course I know him. I work on his plane."

"Does he know Sebastian?"

"Yes. Casually, at least. Most of the pilots meet at some time or another. You don't think—"

"I don't know what to think," Alden said. "I'm just looking for connections, that's all."

"This have to do with that guy who died at the bookstore on Saturday?"

"Why, Chuck, maybe you should be the investigative reporter."

"Ha," Chuck huffed. "No, thanks. But I've seen that guy at the airport. He was hanging out with Blake one day."

"Was he really? That's very interesting."

"Can you keep my name out of your story?"

"No problem." Alden shook his hand. "But I might come back if I have more questions."

"Don't forget my beer." Chuck gave him the stink eye, but his tone was light.

Alden nodded with a smile. "Done. Thanks, man."

He didn't mind buying Chuck a beer or three. He already owed one to Porter Cobb, if the filmmaker ever made it to Comet Cove. Fine. He was going to want a lot of beer when this story was over. Especially when he relived that bounce when the plane hit the lagoon.

He checked his phone when he got back to the car. There was a text from Roz:

I've got to talk to you. You're not going to believe this contract.

And you're not going to believe what I just found out.

I want to know now! But I need to talk to Sheryl. She just walked in. Bean Me Up in 45 minutes?

How about Taco Titan? We didn't have time for breakfast.

Whose fault was that? 🙄 See you there.

chapter
eighteen

"HEY, Sheryl. I thought you were taking the week off." Roz wandered over to the one free desk they left for freelancers who wanted to drop by, though most of them filed remotely. Sheryl seemed to like the companionship of the office, not that any other reporters were there at the moment. Bruce had left, and John was in his fishbowl, on the phone.

Sheryl, in loose tan linen pants and a pink T-shirt patterned with green leaves, looked up from her laptop. "Hi, Roz. I just had to get out of the house, you know? Otherwise I just pace or go outside and start gardening, and if I trim anything more off the plants I have, I'm going to have to plant all new ones." She laughed, a little nervously.

Roz leaned against the desk next to Sheryl's chair. Besides the freelancer's laptop, the surface was empty except for a couple of reference books and the scanner they kept to listen to police calls. There'd been radio chatter when she walked in this morning, but it had stopped almost immediately. She'd been so busy, she forgot to look into what she might've missed. And now Sheryl was here.

"How are you doing?" Roz asked. "Are the police bothering you?"

"Not so much, though they threatened to come talk to me again. I told them I don't know anything else."

"What a pain." Roz paused, aware of how awkward the next couple of minutes were going to be.

Sheryl sat back and looked up at her. "Have—have you learned any more about what happened?"

So maybe *that* was why Sheryl came to the office. And Roz didn't want to answer that question directly.

"We've learned a little more about Wayne," Roz said.

"Oh, really?" Dread colored her question.

"How much do you know about the movies he made?"

Sheryl seemed to relax a little. "Oh, they were really good. They won awards and were in film festivals. Mostly small ones, but he'd done a feature or two."

"So you've seen some of them?"

"Well, no. Except *Fastest Spin Wins*." Sheryl lifted one shoulder in a half shrug. "He said the rights were tied up in sensitive negotiations and that's why they weren't on YouTube or streaming."

There was that phrase again. "He didn't have a copy he could show you?"

"Oh, he did, I'm sure. It just wasn't convenient, I guess. I mean, we always had other things to talk about." Sheryl looked starry-eyed for a second as she pushed her hair away from her face. "Why are you asking?"

"Alden and I have been looking into Wayne, and we think maybe he didn't make all the movies he talked about."

Sheryl's face froze as she blinked up at Roz. "I'm sure that's not true."

"*Are* you sure?" Roz didn't want to be too tough on Sheryl, but how could she be so innocent given her connection to the guy?

"Well, he told me ..." Sheryl's voice trailed off.

"Wayne told people a lot of things," Roz said gently. "How far had he gotten in developing your script?"

"Um, well, he said he had a couple of directors interested. You know this Hollywood stuff. Nothing happens overnight."

"That's what I hear," Roz agreed. "Had you invested in the movie?"

"Just in some preproduction work Wayne said he had to do —a trailer. A pitch deck. Storyboards to get the right actors interested and so on."

And there it was. He should've been paying her as a scriptwriter. Instead, she paid him.

"How much?" Roz asked.

"Oh, um." Sheryl seemed to be catching on. Her voice wavered. "About fifty thousand dollars. But he said I'd make ten times that when the movie got made."

"He said you'd make half a million dollars? That's—a lot." Some writers made that, but it was way more than a first-time scriptwriter could expect unless they'd written a huge block-buster, at least according to stuff she'd googled.

"I know! I was so excited." Sheryl paused, her enthusiasm fading. "And he was so nice to me. So sweet. We were going to go on a trip together, just the two of us. He's the first man I've seriously dated since the divorce." A tear rolled down her cheek.

Now Roz felt terrible. "I'm sorry."

"So am I." Sheryl sniffled and turned back to the laptop, though Roz wondered if she could even see the screen through her now copious tears. Sheryl might be sorry in more ways than one as she thought about what Roz said.

That weasel Wayne Vandershell had bilked Sheryl out of fifty thousand dollars. Even if he'd intended to use the money as he said, all of which sounded like a scam, he'd lied about his credentials. Was she his only mark?

And was Sheryl as innocent as she seemed? Roz sat at her desk and snuck a look at her. If Sheryl had figured out Wayne was a weasel, did she kill him?

Roz had just closed her laptop when her phone vibrated. She eyed the ID and picked it up. "Duke? What's up?"

"How are you doing today? You could've died yesterday."

"Well aware," Roz said, speaking softly so Sheryl couldn't hear. "I'm fine, though I threw out those clothes. Thanks for the ride. Any more word on Vandershell?"

"If you mean the autopsy, nothing more than I already told you." He sounded strangely excited. "I'm surprised I didn't hear from you this morning."

Oh, crap. The scanner. "What happened?"

"I really shouldn't tell you this, but the sheriff is putting out a press release at noon. I'm letting you get a head start, but please wait till then to publish it."

"What?" Roz stuck the phone between her ear and shoulder and opened up her laptop again, ready to type.

"The department sent a tow truck to roll Wayne Vandershell's BMW off Main Street today—we didn't even realize it was there until it got a couple of parking tickets—and the driver found something funny under the seat."

"What, Duke? Drugs? An eight-track player? What?"

He laughed. "There were some odd wires and—long story short, the driver called us before he tried to move it. Deputy Byrd took one look and called in the county bomb squad. There was a bomb under the seat rigged to explode with a remote trigger. Plastic explosives."

Roz said something very unladylike, and Duke sniggered.

"Did it blow up?" she asked, even as she realized it was a dumb question. She probably would've heard it if it had.

"Disarmed. It's being analyzed. No leads yet. But somebody *really* wanted Wayne Vandershell dead. Oh, and that book you left me? There was blood on it."

"THANK GOD YOU'RE HERE. I'm starving," Alden said as Roz slipped into his booth at Taco Titan. It was a chronically packed low-class Tex-Mex place with colorful paper garlands and a llama piñata and an inflatable Corona airplane (he didn't really want that looming over him right now) and a digital wall clock counting down to Cinco de Mayo. Less than a month until the worst amateur drinking holiday of the year, but he loved it anyway.

And he loved Roz.

She was glowing, full of news. "I'm hungry, too. I almost forgot to eat."

"I never forget to eat." He'd already made a dent in the chips and salsa. He grinned and pushed a menu toward her. "I ordered you a Coke."

"Works for me," she said. "I'm getting the Taco Tuesday special."

They both did, rattling off their orders for the taco platter to the server, who'd brought Roz's soda in a huge cup.

"I had to type up a quick story for online," she said after the server left, "embargoed till the sheriff's press release came out. John was going to push the button."

Alden sat up straighter. "Are they releasing something on the cause of death?"

"Nope." She looked at her watch, then at him, mischief in her eyes. "It should be live now."

"Aw, you're not going to tell me?" He was already pulling out his phone and went to the *Courier-Beacon* site. *No way!* "Someone tried to blow up Wayne Vandershell? You've got to be kidding me. Somebody really wanted that guy dead."

"That's exactly what Duke said."

He gave her a flat-lipped expression that made her laugh. "Well, I have news too."

"And I have more news! You first."

Alden outlined what Chuck told him about the Cessna's avgas being contaminated with jet fuel, likely the cause of the plane's engine croaking.

"So not an accident," Roz guessed.

"Who knows how the NTSB will see it, but Chuck says there's no way Sebastian accidentally added jet fuel to the tank. Someone did it deliberately."

"So somebody might be trying to kill Sebastian, too. That makes my news all the more interesting."

"What?" Alden said, and then the tacos arrived. They took a moment to get a bite in their bellies before she replied.

"These al pastor tacos are so addictive." She sipped her cola.

"Roz," he said impatiently and set out to finish the first of three crunchy beef tacos.

She smiled. "Oh, all right. Sebastian and Wayne's agreement included an escrow fund, the one that Sebastian thought Wayne wasn't contributing to. They both had to put in a substantial amount to ensure the health of the movie studio project. Even more interesting given what happened, there was a death clause. If one of them died, the entire escrow fund went to the other partner."

"Wow. How much are we talking here?"

"This paperwork didn't include exact numbers, but it had to be a lot for a big project like this one, right?" she said. "That's not all. If Sebastian died first, Wayne would've had the right to buy the property from his estate for far below market value, which I suppose was a way to ensure the project would continue. That way all of Wayne's so-called investment wouldn't have been lost."

"That sounds like a terrible agreement from Sebastian's point of view. How could he sign that?"

Roz offered a half shrug. "Maybe he did it for love. He said Wayne agreed to make one of Nicole's screenplays into a film and that's why he went along. And I think he was charmed by the guy, at least at first. Sebastian seemed to be excited by the prospect of a movie studio, too."

"But if Wayne hadn't paid his fair share to the escrow fund when he died, that means Sebastian is really out of luck. Though he couldn't have known that up front if Wayne's shady lawyer was hiding the truth." Alden forked up a tasty bite of refried beans and considered the ramifications. "What if both of them died?"

"That's a good question. The heir of the last one to die would make out. The inheritor would be the rightful owner of everything—the property, the project, the money."

"Holy cannoli. We need to see if Wayne has an heir."

"I wonder if Duke found family to notify. An heir is certainly a potential suspect. But Sebastian would've theoretically benefited from Wayne's death. And then if Sebastian died ..." Roz pursed her lips around her straw and drank deeply of her soda, and Alden got distracted by her mouth until she said, "I think we know who Sebastian's heir is. Nicole."

"Whoa." He paused for a second, then resumed eating. They both did, chewing on the idea.

"Have you talked to Nicole yet?" he finally asked, all three tacos happily consumed.

"Not yet."

"If Nicole killed Wayne and then sabotaged her husband's plane ..."

"That's heavy," Roz said. "Killing her own husband? The father of her children? But she's not our only suspect. Wayne was no good. He ticked people off. He bilked Sheryl out of fifty thousand dollars—that we know of. "

"Good lord. How?"

"He asked her to 'invest' in a pitch deck and a trailer and stuff like that for a movie he probably wasn't making."

"And she was naive enough to go along." Alden hated seeing people ripped off, especially when scammers preyed on their fragile egos and dreams. "Do you think she did it?"

Roz swirled her cup. "Honestly, no. I think she's just starting to realize he wasn't all he pretended to be. But maybe. We thought she found the body. Maybe he wasn't dead yet when she went to see him."

Alden's phone buzzed on the table, and he eyed the text. "That's Craig getting back to me. He says he can meet me at Bean Me Up. He's there working."

"I'll go with you." Roz dabbed her mouth with her napkin and smiled. "Mocha for dessert. I could go for that. Maybe we'll learn more about Enolia and Wayne. Then we'll deal with Nicole."

"And Blake," Alden added.

"Right, Blake. Our flying thespian. Alden?"

"Yes?" He reached across the table impulsively. She laid her hand in his, and he grasped it.

"Let's tread carefully," she murmured. "Somebody tried to kill Wayne in more ways than one. And somebody tried to kill Sebastian, too."

"And us!" He feigned an affronted tone. "You can't leave us out."

She let out a dry chuckle. "I suspect we were collateral damage, but that's kind of my point. If the killer or killers decide we're getting too close, I have no doubt they'll try to kill again. And they might actually aim at us next time."

"I won't let them hurt you." He squeezed her hand. "And I won't let either of us get into a plane until this is all over."

chapter
nineteen

"BOTH OF YOU. HOW NICE."

Roz couldn't mistake Craig's sarcastic tone as he greeted Roz and Alden in Bean Me Up. He sat at the long, tall table in front of the windows that let guests watch the street as they sipped. Or worked, as Craig was apparently doing, given the laptop open in front of him. Alden had left his computer in his car, but Roz had hers, just in case.

Craig had shed his bow tie but still wore his wire-rimmed spectacles, and the afternoon light shone gently off his mostly bald head.

"Thanks for seeing us," Alden said cheerfully. Roz hid her smile. Alden was so great at swaggering into a situation no matter how hostile it was. "We'll order a coffee, and then we'll be right with you."

"Not a problem." Craig turned back to his keyboard as if they weren't there, so Alden and Roz ordered their regular brews from Lily. They went back to the table to wait, taking seats on the stools opposite Craig, spoiling his view of Main Street.

"Working on anything interesting?" Roz asked, pulling a pen and notebook from her bag.

"Research for Enolia's next novel," Craig said.

"Ooo, what about?" Alden was keen and friendly.

"If I told you, I'd have to kill you." Craig closed the computer to emphasize it was none of their business. Not that Roz had X-ray eyes like the guy in that movie Blake mentioned. "And no, I would never put that phrase in a book. It's too much of a cliché."

"Do you write?" Alden asked. "I mean, besides research?"

Craig's nose twitched. "I do. Fiction. Screenplays."

The next question was obvious. "Were you working with Wayne Vandershell, too?" Roz asked.

Craig sipped his half-finished coffee. It looked foamy. Latte, maybe? "He asked to see my work, but I felt it was a conflict of interest since I work for Enolia. My job is to ensure her work is perfect."

Now that was an interesting statement. Wasn't making the work perfect the superstar writer's job? But maybe this was how Craig made himself feel important.

"Do you edit Enolia's books?" Roz asked.

"I—no. Her agent and editors at her publisher do that. I have early input on her work."

"Research," Alden said, repeating what Craig had told them.

"Yes, research," Craig replied, though his mouth twitched as if he wanted to say more.

Then Alden looked up and smiled at Lily, their cute blond barista, who appeared at that moment to deliver his black coffee and Roz's mocha.

"Thanks, Lily." Roz took the warm paper cup and set it down as she waited for it to cool to non-lava levels.

"No problem." Lily took in their coffee klatch with a curious gaze, but she headed back to the counter.

"How did Enolia find you?" Roz asked Craig.

"I worked at the library near her home in Upstate New York."

"So you trained as a librarian?" Alden asked.

"Trained, yes, once I decided computer science wasn't for me. I didn't have the full library sciences degree. But she found me at the research desk nine years ago. I loved her books, and I helped her so much, I turned out to be indispensable." Craig smiled. This guy loved his job.

"What book did she first have you do research on?" Alden asked.

Craig looked out the window for a few seconds. "Was it *The Wentletrap* or—" He turned back to Alden. "No, it was *The Calico Killer*."

"Like the Calico Cat?" Roz asked.

Craig gave her a disdainful look. "Like a calico scallop shell. There are shells in all her titles. At least all the beach thrillers."

"Oh." So *The Murex Murder* was named for a murex shell. She should've known. "Clever."

Craig adjusted his glasses, and his pleasant mien returned. "She hired me full-time after that. I didn't have any ties that were important to me there, so I traveled with her and became her assistant in all things."

All things covered a lot of ground. But that meant he should know a lot about Enolia and her dealings with Wayne Vandershell.

"So you saw a lot of Wayne?" Alden asked, obviously thinking along the same lines.

Craig cocked his head. "Why are you asking?"

"We're interested in his connection to Enolia. I'm writing a feature about her," Alden said, "but we're also writing about Wayne Vandershell's unfortunate death."

Craig snorted softly and replied to Alden, "Yes, I saw a lot of Wayne. More than enough. She was quite taken with him."

"And you didn't approve?" Roz guessed.

Craig turned to her and sidestepped the question. "She is welcome to play with whomever she likes, and she liked him a lot. After all, he was going to adapt her book, maybe books, for the screen."

Roz and Alden exchanged a glance, then Roz took a sweet sip of her mocha as Alden said, "We think Wayne might have exaggerated his credentials. Did you think he was sincere when it came to Enolia?"

Craig gave him a cool, steady look through those round glasses. "I don't think 'sincerity' was something he specialized in."

Ouch! Roz thought.

"But Enolia didn't really care," Craig continued. "As I said, she enjoyed his company. And she was excited about seeing her work in a movie or TV, however it played out."

"How far along did they get in turning the books into movies?" Alden asked.

"I'm not sure," Craig admitted. "Wayne said he had interest from Netflix for a movie or series, and he also had a few screenwriters he was talking to about adaptations."

Alden's eyebrows lifted. "He could've talked to you."

"He knew I wasn't interested. And he said he had some big names in the queue."

"Did he ask Enolia to invest in the project?" Roz asked, taking notes.

"I believe he did." Craig's tone set off Roz's internal lie

detector. "But she didn't want to share the details. So that is *not* on the record."

He knew a lot more than he was saying. Roz was sure of it. But he wanted to protect Enolia, his bread and butter. She understood that, too.

"Mae Middleton told me that Enolia is her aunt," Alden said, "and had promised Mae some money for the bookstore. Do you know about that?"

Craig's light brown eyes flashed—in anger or frustration, she couldn't say—and then he was back to his calm assistant persona. "That bookstore is a money pit. But Enolia loves her niece and wants her to be happy, so she will give her what she needs. That's the kind of person she is. And since Enolia won't have her money tied up with Wayne now, Mae won't have to worry. Not that I know about any money Enolia might have given to Wayne."

Roz held back an eye roll. "Was her gift to the bookstore ever in question?"

"It isn't now." A classic non-answer.

Roz contained a sigh. Craig was in full armor now, the knight defending his queen. When Alden glanced at her, she shot him a resigned smile, and he turned back to Craig.

"We really appreciate your time." Alden slid a business card across the table. "If you think of anything we should know, please call or email me."

"Of course," Craig said, though his tone said anything but. "When will the feature run on Enolia?"

"I'm not sure," Alden said as Roz answered, "Friday."

Alden smiled. "I'm trying to get some extra time, but my editor is tough on me."

"Take all the time you need," Craig said. "She wouldn't want you to rush."

"If only you were my editor," Alden joked, and Roz lightly smacked his arm. A corner of Craig's mouth lifted.

Enolia's right-hand man watched them as they ambled to the exit, and only then did he reopen his laptop.

The reporters stepped outside with a jingle of the door.

"Walk with me," Alden said.

"Good idea." Roz didn't want anyone—especially Craig—to overhear them. Or read their lips.

It was a beautiful, breezy day, and several people were out shopping and enjoying the fair weather. And it felt good just to walk. She spent too much time behind a desk.

"How much of that was true?" she asked when they'd walked past a few businesses.

"Maybe all of it, but it's what he left out that bothers me."

"I'm sure he knows more about the money," she said.

"I thought that too."

"How much do you think Wayne tried to get out of Enolia?" Roz asked.

"How much did he *actually* get?" Alden mused. "And was she completely clueless?"

"If Enolia thought Wayne stole from her, she might've wanted to do him harm." Roz sipped her mocha. "She writes murder books for a living. Suppose she sabotaged his vape pen?"

"Or had a fight with him in the alley? We found that book that might be hers out there. And Mae said something about Enolia complaining of a spot on her dress. But of course, if Enolia was anywhere near him when the pen blew up, there would've been more than a little stain."

"Yuck."

Alden lifted one shoulder. "Sorry. It's yucky. And I know

she writes murder books, but I just can't see it. She's a writer, not a fighter."

"And you're a poet and didn't know it."

"Oh, I know it, baby." Alden grinned at her.

Roz tossed him a flirty look. "I'm still waiting for my first poem from you."

"It'll probably come sooner than the novel," he admitted.

She chuckled. "I found it interesting what he implied about the money Enolia planned to give to Mae."

"That the funds Enolia might have fed to Wayne could've meant Mae wasn't getting her bailout? But now that Wayne's dead, Mae's in the money? You know what that means."

"Unfortunately, yes." Roz glanced across the street toward Big Bang Books. "Mae benefited significantly from Wayne's death, because her aunt now has the money to give to her. Doesn't Enolia Honeywood have tons of money anyway?"

"One would think," Alden said, "but how much of it is available at any given time?"

"Wayne must've asked for a big chunk. And Mae might've needed a bunch to save the bookstore. If Wayne kept asking, he could've bled Enolia dry. His death stopped the gravy train and gave Mae what she needed."

"That's motive for murder, but nothing Craig said about the money is on the record," he said.

"OK, I guess all we got out of that interview that we can print is that Wayne promised to get Enolia's books on film. Which we already knew. But we need to think about Mae's role in all this."

"Maybe I can get more out of Craig later. And I'm going to shoot an email to someone I know at Netflix, see if there's anything to what he said about Wayne's claim of developing adaptations of Enolia's books there. In the meantime, I have to talk to Blake."

"Mind if I come along?"

"What about Nicole?" Alden stopped walking.

"Nicole *and* Sebastian. I want to talk to both of them."

"Wait. I should come with you when you see Nicole. Just in case she's a homicidal maniac."

Roz quirked her mouth at him. "I can handle it. But it might be fun to have you along. John told me to go out and nail this story with you, so I say we do it."

"He said I should nail you?" he teased. "We should do it?"

She smacked his arm again. "Men!"

He snickered. "Can't live with us, can't kill us."

"Unless you're Wayne Vandershell," Roz said. "Somebody killed him, one way or another."

"And we still don't know who," he said. "Let's track down Blake."

chapter
twenty

A WOMAN ANSWERED when Alden called Blake's house, but to his disappointment, it wasn't Lexie Wintergarten. He'd know the actress's voice anywhere. Instead, he was pretty sure it was some sort of housekeeper, and when Alden explained who he was and that he and Blake were tight, she was unimpressed, said Blake was playing golf, and hung up without offering to take a message.

"He's got to be at Vesper Lakes," Alden said as Roz drove them south from downtown in her silver hatchback.

"Of course he's at Vesper Lakes."

Alden still stung from his inability to charm the housekeeper. "There's that little municipal course up north, but that doesn't seem like his speed."

"He's probably practicing for the celebrity golf tournament coming up this weekend," Roz said. "Maybe it's better that we talk to him with a bunch of people around."

"You're not worried about Blake, are you?"

Roz shot him a sidelong glance as she navigated to Highway A1A. "For one thing, he knows about airplanes. But I can't figure out why he'd want to kill Sebastian Esquivel, unless

Sebastian's problems with the movie studio were somehow standing in the way of Blake's big comeback."

"At the very least, he might be able to tell us when and why Wayne was at the airport. Chuck said Wayne was hanging around with Blake there one day."

"He was? You didn't tell me that," Roz said accusingly.

"I had so much other stuff to tell you!"

"True," she acknowledged as she turned south on A1A toward the inlet bridge. "But doesn't that make Blake even more suspicious? Maybe he and Wayne were working together to screw over Sebastian."

"You have an evil mind." But Alden loved it when she got going.

"I'm just good at imagining other people's evil minds." As if to prove her point, she went on, "Even if Blake didn't have it out for Sebastian, he might've wanted to kill Wayne. Blake didn't tell us he'd given Wayne money, but I'd bet anything he did, and for what? He's probably angry at Wayne for telling him he was going to cast him in some nonexistent movie."

"We can't go in there all guns blazing at Blake. Maybe there *was* a movie project. We don't know for sure. Have you talked to Duke lately? He might know if Wayne had a laptop, and that should tell us what he was really working on."

"After he told me about the book—"

"What book?"

"The one you found in the alley. It had blood on it."

"Ha!" Alden said. "And you accuse me of withholding information."

Roz chortled. "It's a lot of moving parts, OK? Anyway, Duke confirmed Wayne was renting a furnished beach condo, short-term. He didn't say there was a computer, but I can't imagine there wasn't. Now that we know more, I'll ask him if he found any evidence of movie deals or money changing hands. Oh, and the only family he has is an estranged father who lives in California and has been on a European trip for the past two weeks. Probably not the killer."

"Did Wayne have a will? Maybe Sheryl's the beneficiary and she'll get all her money back."

"Unlikely." Roz sounded amused. "But I'll ask."

"Think Duke will tell you?"

"Well, he does like me," Roz said coyly.

"Not as much as he used to."

She guffawed. "You're funny. But probably right."

"He knows the score." Alden had made no secret that Roz was his, and Duke damn well knew it. "But I suppose he likes you enough if he told you about the bomb before they released the news."

"I told you, we're old friends."

"Uh-huh."

Roz giggled. And that made him laugh. She made his heart lighter. And that was a precious thing in this crazy world.

As she drove, he sent an email to his source at Netflix, who got back to him five minutes later. "No Enolia Honeywood properties in the works," his response said. "But they'd make great movies. Interesting thought. Thanks, Knox."

He told Roz about it as she turned in to the scenic driveway of Vesper Lakes.

The recently expanded golf club sat on the southeast side of Comet Cove, well beyond the inlet but not quite as far south as the airport. It had no view of the ocean, but it shouldered into the wildlife preserve that the Esquivel family had donated to the town, the same one the city was working to make accessible to the public.

Vesper Lakes Golf Club was anything but wild. It was

pretty, Alden had to admit, with its rolling emerald fairways, water hazards (the aspirational "lakes"), clumps of oaks and palm trees, and sprawling, stone-accented clubhouse. A driving range and other practice areas had been added to the club's original footprint. The grounds were huge, with lots of space for audiences and media when they came, and the founders of Vesper Lakes very much wanted them to come. They'd already had one regional tournament that drew several Florida pros, and the celebrity event this weekend should garner a lot of publicity as they cultivated their connections to the pro circuit.

The last time Alden had seen it up close, he and Roz were clawing their way back to civilization after an unwanted adventure, and the place was in shambles. Now construction was over, and it was a pristine testament to the power of money and excessive irrigation.

As Roz pulled into the parking lot, he texted the golf pro who sometimes fed him gems. When Roz turned off the car, Alden had his answer. "Blake's at the outdoor bar."

"How do you *do* that?" she asked, but she was smiling.

"I buy a lot of guys a lot of beers."

They got out and headed toward the grand entrance.

The porte cochere could offer shade and rain protection to any number of fancy cars or golf carts idling on the pavered driveway, though the valets were wrangling only a couple of European imports. An actor Alden recognized got into one of them. And they saw a couple of other minor celebrities in the airy lobby, where they ran into a familiar face among the wide soft chairs and forest of potted palms.

"Hi, Hai," Roz said to their photographer, who had his bag on his shoulder and a camera around his neck.

"Hi, hi, hi," Hai said back. "Are you writing about the celebrity golf tournament too?"

"Uh, no. Is Tim here?" she asked.

"He just left."

"How were the nudists?" Alden asked.

"Lightly broiled," Hai said. "Thank God they had big signs. Got some good stuff though. I was about to go back to the office and file."

"Hey," Alden said, "would you mind getting a photo of Blake Burbage first? I hear he's at the bar."

"Already got a couple of him," the photographer said. "I took photos of all the teams for the tournament, at least of the people who are in town."

"Great. Don't let us keep you." Roz waved him away, then gave Alden a knowing look as Hai left. She was right about Blake being in the celebrity golf tournament.

"Smarty pants," Alden acknowledged. "Sign says it's this way."

They passed more signs indicating locker rooms and the pro shop, then passed the restaurant and entered the bar. It was dark inside and full of golf memorabilia, but outside, the covered patio was bright and comfortable, with its own bar and several tables. Blake was at the bar with another guy. A comedian Alden had seen on TV.

Comet Cove was so weird.

The comedian shook hands with Blake and walked around them as they approached the bar.

Blake's eyebrows lifted in surprise. "It's the free press."

"Free roving, at least for now," Alden said. "I'm surprised no one threw us out."

Blake smiled. "Are you here to talk to the golfers? I already talked to one of your guys. He's nice."

"Tim is great," Roz said. "We're actually here about something else. Can we sit for a minute?"

Blake gestured to the barstools. Roz left the stool next to the actor empty, which Alden took as an invitation.

"Can I buy you another one?" Alden asked, gesturing to Blake's bottle.

"Nonalcoholic beer. It's all I drink these days. I'm good. You want something?" He looked to Roz, then back to Alden. "Or do you want to ask me something else about Wayne Vandershell?"

Alden lifted his hands, palms up. "Busted."

A bartender wandered over with a look in his eye that suggested they should buy something or get out. So Alden ordered a Bohemia Brewing IPA.

Roz raised an eyebrow at him and ordered a club soda with lime.

"So." Alden turned back to Blake. "We had an interesting day yesterday."

"Crashing in Sebastian's plane? Interesting is one way to put it." Blake sipped his brew and eyed him with amusement.

"So you know Sebastian?" Roz asked.

Blake nodded. "I know him slightly from hanging out at the airport. I was surprised when Wayne introduced him to me as his development partner for the movie studio."

"Who initiated your airport meetup?" Alden asked.

Blake looked taken aback by the question. Then he thought for a minute while Alden took a refreshing sip of his newly arrived beer.

"I think Wayne suggested that visit," Blake said. "Yeah, he did. Said he was doing research on small airplanes. One of his associates was writing about a pilot in a script, and he wanted to make sure she got the facts right. A character wanted to harm the pilot by messing with his plane. Something like that. I think Wayne just wanted a free plane ride."

Alden tried not to sound too eager. "Did he say who was writing about sabotaging a plane?"

"No." Blake's eyes widened. "Sebastian's plane wasn't—"

"We'll find out when the NTSB does." Alden didn't want him to know how much they knew.

"How much did you tell Wayne about sabotaging a plane?" Roz asked.

Blake chuckled. "I told him to use Google. I'm not trying to bring my plane down. I'm trying to keep it in the air. Fortunately, the airport has a great mechanic who's usually there—Chuck Teague."

"I know Chuck," Alden said.

Blake gestured with his bottle. "I told Wayne that Chuck might be a good guy to ask, too."

Chuck would know how to tamper with a plane. Of course he would.

"And you gave Wayne a ride?" Roz was asking.

"Sure, why not? The guy was going to produce my big comeback script, remember?" Blake's voice was full of irony.

"How much did he ask you to invest?" Alden said. Sometimes it made sense to ask the direct question rather than dance around it.

Blake clunked his bottle down on the bar. "So we're talking about money now?"

"It's relevant," Alden said. "He got one of his stable of writers to give him a significant amount of money, and we think he had no plans to use it to help her get her movie made. We're wondering how many people he might have tapped for funds."

Blake blew out a breath. "Oh, he tapped me, and I paid.

But I'm not happy to hear he had no intention of carrying through." He seemed genuinely disturbed.

"How much?" Roz asked in a soft voice that would've had Alden confessing everything.

Blake picked at the label on his bottle. "Not that much to start with, though I said I'd give him more."

Roz just sat there looking at him, lips pursed around the straw in her tall glass, sipping. Waiting.

Blake tipped his head from side to side. "In the ballpark of a quarter million."

Not that much? Alden wanted to scream. Why did he get into journalism again? Oh, right. Because he wanted to change the world and leave the family fortune behind. Even if he had a chunk of it set aside for rainy days.

"Any chance you'll get your investment back now that Wayne is gone?" Roz asked Blake.

Blake shrugged, but the set of his jaw suggested he wasn't as nonchalant as he wanted to appear. "My lawyer is looking into it. We had a contract."

"Well, I hope you get it back." Alden took another sip of his glass of beer and set it on the bar, half full. They had a long day ahead of them, and they had to get going. He plucked cash out of his now-dry wallet—cash was old-fashioned, but when he was fishing for gossip, it was useful—and laid it on the bar to pay for the drinks. "I'd like to check in with you again if we find out more. Would that be OK?"

"I'd like to know more," Blake said evenly. "Have a good day."

"Thank you." Roz slipped off her stool and shook Blake's hand.

Alden did likewise, and they headed out of the bar and into the parking lot.

"Holy crap," she said once they got into her car.

"No kidding," Alden replied. "One of Wayne's stable of writers was allegedly working on a script about sabotaging a plane? Who?"

"A 'she,' according to what Blake told us."

"They were all 'shes,'" Alden said.

"He made deals with men, too, but they weren't writers." Roz started up the car. "We still don't know how many scribes he had on the hook. But we do know about Sheryl. Enolia. And then there's the one who's married to the pilot whose plane went down."

Alden buckled up, in more ways than one. "I guess it's time to talk to Nicole Esquivel."

chapter
twenty-one

"I WANT to see if Sebastian is at home before we go." Roz picked up her phone and cranked the car's AC while they sat in the golf club parking lot. "I'd like to talk to Nicole and Sebastian together if possible."

"For safety?" Alden asked.

"Just to—I mean, it's not my business whether they talk to each other or not, but if they clear the air in front of us, it helps us, too." She typed out a text.

"You mean if he confesses he got into the movie studio deal to further her career?"

"Right, because I don't think she knows about that. And maybe she'll tell us more about Wayne."

A moment later, she got a text back from Sebastian. "He's on a work site, unfortunately. I think we'll have to face Nicole on her own. Possibly with small children."

"I'm fine with killer mommy. It's the kids that scare me."

Roz laughed. Was Alden speaking in code? Was he scared of kids—of having kids? Oh, hell, she wasn't too keen on the idea yet either. But never say never.

They reached the Esquivels' Saturn Shores neighborhood

within fifteen minutes. Construction was in progress next to the old gatehouse.

"I believe they're rebuilding the guest gates," she said. "I knew the HOA approved it, but there was nothing here yesterday."

"Gates aren't much help if you live with your killer," Alden observed.

"Let's not get ahead of ourselves." She eased past the workers, exchanging courtesy waves with them.

The McMansions looked extra chunky in the bright light and shadow of midafternoon. The canals sparkled, the boats gleaming at their docks. Palm trees twinkled as the strong breeze angled their fronds to the sun. And then they were at the Esquivels' ostentatious pile.

It was funny, Roz thought. They didn't seem like pretentious people. She was a busy mom trying to have a creative career on the side. He was a dorky collector of baseball memorabilia who liked to fly when he wasn't building more McMansions. A builder couldn't live in a cottage, she supposed. This house was a calling card.

They took the long walk around the front to the sheltered entrance.

"That's some door," Alden said as the doorbell that evoked cathedral bells pealed inside.

There was movement behind the dark doors' leaded-glass circle. After a painful few seconds of Roz wondering whether they'd be left on the stoop like an unwanted newspaper, one half opened.

"Roz?" Nicole asked. Her blond hair was up again but falling out of the clip, blobs of something yellow stained her threadbare Green Day T-shirt, and she wore faded blue yoga pants and flip-flops. Kids yelled, and the TV blared in the background.

"Hey, Nicole. I wonder if we could chat for a minute? I texted Sebastian, but he said he was busy. Oh, and this is Alden Knox, another reporter at *The Courier-Beacon*."

Nicole took a second to focus, then smiled up at Alden. It was hard not to. He was so darn handsome. But then her eyes flickered, wary.

"Very nice to meet you," Alden said.

"Listen, this isn't a great time," Nicole said. "Mateo got home half an hour ago, and the kids got into my secret candy stash, and their heads are about to pop off."

Alden exchanged a quick look with Roz. "I could entertain them while Roz talks with you for a minute, if that's all right."

Roz and Nicole both stared at him.

Nicole brightened. "OK, great!"

Roz wished she didn't have to talk to Nicole, because she would really like to see Alden entertaining the three hellions. Though maybe it wasn't fair to call the little one a hellion yet. Imp in training? She shot him an *Are you sure?* look, and he just smiled back.

OK. We're doing this.

Nicole led them left through the house toward the open kitchen with its modern glass pendant lights and a bank of oversize stainless-steel appliances. A wide, curving granite counter that doubled as an eating area marked the boundary between the kitchen and a spacious living space with a big television (showing *Bluey*) and comfy furniture. It seemed the whole space was a play area, with colorful toys scattered everywhere.

"I'll make coffee. Do you like coffee?" Nicole asked.

"If it's not too much trouble," Roz said.

"Is the Keurig all right? It's easy." As opposed to the huge chrome coffee contraption sitting by the stove. "What do you drink?"

"Oh, anything. Bean Me Up spoils me with mochas, but I'm good with whatever you have." Roz didn't need more coffee, but being friendly never hurt. And, really, she *did* always need more coffee.

"I have a chocolate-flavored coffee," Nicole said, looking through a bin of various tiny cuplets.

"Sounds great."

"I'm fine," Alden said. "Do you want to introduce me to the kids?"

"Sure." Nicole got the machine started, then called for the children's attention. "Kids, this is Alden. Why don't you show him a game while Ms. Roz and I talk?"

"Alden can be the horse!" Gabriela screamed.

"I'm the knight!" Mateo hollered. "He's a bad horse!"

Roz had to bite her lip so she wouldn't laugh.

Diego ignored them all and sucked on a giant Lego block while watching *Bluey* from a pillow on the floor.

Alden grinned at Roz, then walked over to the area in front of the TV.

"Get down, horse!" Gabriela ordered.

Alden groaned a little as he lowered himself to his hands and knees. "Like this?"

"I'll get the sword!" Mateo exclaimed.

Roz gave in and laughed, then followed Nicole back into the kitchen area, where the coffee maker had finished hissing and spitting. Nicole handed the blue-glazed pottery mug to Roz, grabbed her own cup and beckoned to her to follow.

Alden neighed.

The women ended up on a covered back patio, complete

with its own outdoor kitchen and fire table. Enclosed in a big screened cage, the patio and swimming pool overlooked the dock and lagoon.

"It's like a resort," Roz said. "Really nice."

"It is. I wish I had more time to enjoy it. But I'm so busy with the kids."

"And your writing." Roz sat in a cushioned chair catty-corner to Nicole's, in front of a coffee table topped with polished marble. "Sebastian told us you liked to write."

"Oh my God. Sebastian." Tears came to Nicole's eyes. "I'm so glad you two are OK."

So she wasn't glad Sebastian was OK? Or maybe that was implied.

"It was scary, but he's a good pilot," Roz said. "We were fine."

"You were asking him questions about the movie studio project?"

Who was interviewing who? "Yes, we were. And about his partner, Wayne Vandershell."

Nicole's blue eyes darkened. "That bastard."

Roz sputtered on a sip of coffee. She swallowed. "Why do you say that?"

"Because he was ripping off Sebastian." Whoa. Nicole was really angry.

Roz played dumb. "Ripping off?"

"Getting his sleazy lawyer to certify he'd paid into the escrow when he hadn't. Not matching Seb's twenty-five million dollars. Sticking Sebastian with the bills. And Sebastian is always so nice, he didn't question anything until he was in it neck-deep. It's partly my fault. I never should have introduced them."

Twenty-five million! That wasn't chump change.

Roz had a hunch. "Is there some other reason you're angry with Wayne?"

Nicole leaned forward, set her mug on the coffee table and idly used one finger to spin it around by the handle. "I don't know if I want to talk about this."

"You're worried about it going in the paper?"

Nicole startled as if she just realized she was talking to a reporter. Then she sighed. "You know what? I don't care. He was an awful person. Wayne came on to me. More than once. All while telling me he was going to produce my screenplay. He asked me to invest tens of thousands of dollars in some promotional materials and told me not to tell Sebastian. Said this was 'just between us.' Did he think I was an idiot?"

Roz was on the verge of stunned. Nicole knew a lot more than Sebastian thought she did. And Wayne hit on her? Gross.

"You didn't invest?" Roz slid her notebook out of her bag and started scribbling the high points.

"No, I did not! Why would I invest when Sebastian had already sunk so much money into the studio?"

Roz asked gently, "Why do you think he sunk so much money into the studio?"

Nicole pursed her lips. "He must've thought Wayne would produce my screenplay if he did. It's just the sort of super nice thing Sebastian would do. But I wish he was a little more savvy sometimes."

"Uh-huh." *Holy Tinseltown!* "And Wayne didn't make any progress on producing your screenplay?"

"No, he didn't. And I don't think that was just because I refused to sleep with him or give him my money. I think it was by design. You know what? I think Wayne was full of horse poop." Nicole's kid-friendly non-curse almost made Roz smile. "I found out he talked to other people in the book club—you know, the one at Big Bang Books?—who were screenwriters, too. We have a little writing group there. He had them all going."

"You mean they contributed to his screenplay scheme?"

"You know it's a scheme, don't you?" Nicole's face had a look of satisfaction. "Yes, that's what I mean."

"How many of those writers was he talking to?"

"At least three or four."

Wow. They needed to ask Mae about that. "What is your screenplay about?"

Nicole's eyebrows scrunched together at the question. "It's about a woman who goes on vacation to the beach with her girlfriends and realizes there's more to life than her cranky husband and college-age kids, and she starts over. It's kind of a dramedy."

"So, no airplane stuff?"

"No." Nicole seemed puzzled. "The friends drive to the beach town."

What was Roz supposed to make of that? The story sounded a little like wish fulfillment—ditching the husband and starting over. Though Nicole said Sebastian was really nice. So maybe she didn't want to kill him.

Perhaps more relevant, at least as Nicole told it, the script had nothing to do with sabotaging airplanes.

"Did you ever talk to Blake Burbage?" Roz asked.

Nicole's face softened. "Oh, I'd sure like to. I loved him in *Chain of Honor*!"

"So did I!" Now they were bonding over a TV show. Nicole had good taste.

"Sebastian said Wayne was going to produce a movie at the studio starring Blake." Nicole took another sip of her coffee and looked wistful. "But now that the studio is on ice, I'll probably never get a chance to meet him. I should've talked to him during the signing, but I would feel weird introducing myself to a celebrity, you know?"

So she hated Wayne and didn't know Blake.

"Do you know Chuck Teague?" Roz asked.

Nicole hesitated. "He's the plane mechanic, right? I've met him a couple of times. He seemed OK. A little rough around the edges."

So Roz couldn't rule out an acquaintance with Chuck. Alden seemed to like Chuck, but Chuck also knew how to sabotage airplanes. Would he have done it for Nicole? Or someone else?

There was one more thing she had to ask. "On Saturday, when you took the kids to the bookstore bathroom, you left them alone for a few minutes."

Nicole froze with her coffee cup halfway to her mouth. "What is this? Are you accusing me of child neglect?"

"No! No, of course not. Mateo told me he was in charge."

Nicole rolled her eyes and took a sip and set down her cup again. "He's adorable, isn't he? I was only gone a minute."

"Did you happen to see Wayne, by chance?"

Nicole's face shifted. The wariness returned to her eyes. "I didn't hurt him, if that's what you're asking."

"What? I mean, what did you see? What did you say to him? Did you arrange to meet him?" *She'd gone to see Wayne Vandershell!*

"No! I—I was aware he was at the store and saw him heading to the back hallway. I knew he smoked. When I had to take the kids to the bathroom, I figured it gave me a chance to give him a piece of my mind. I went to the back door, but someone had beaten me to it. So I returned to the bathroom to deal with the kids, which took a while. And then after I took them back into the store, there was that scream, and I heard what happened." Nicole shuddered.

"Wait a second." Roz's heart beat faster. "Someone had beaten you to it? Was Wayne dead?"

"No, of course not! Someone else was yelling at him. I figured I'd wait my turn. And then it was too late."

Roz took a sip of coffee to ease her nerves and make sure she didn't screw this up. Then she posed her question. "Someone else was yelling at him? Who?"

"Enolia Honeywood."

twenty-two

"ENOLIA WAS SCREAMING at Wayne in the alley before her book signing?" Alden asked. Roz had briefed him as she drove them away from the Esquivel house. And just in time, too. He rubbed his head where Mateo had battered him with a plastic sword. "What did she say when she was yelling at him?"

"Nicole didn't know or didn't remember. She says she bowed out before she was seen, and she never saw Wayne again."

"Holy cannoli. If she's telling the truth, she didn't kill Wayne Vandershell."

"But Enolia might've," Roz said. "She might have hit him, at least. And Enolia hung out with Wayne—had access to him. She could've sabotaged the vape pen. Maybe she planted the bomb."

"That's a lot," Alden said.

"I know." A corner of her mouth lifted. "I don't really believe it either. But I'd like to know why she was ticked off at Wayne."

"Even Sebastian might've attacked Wayne. He could have

driven through that alley on the way to pick up Nicole and the kids and seen an opportunity. He certainly had reasons."

"Twenty-five million reasons. But would he have also messed with the vape pen and planted a bomb?" she asked.

"He's pretty technical. He's a pilot. He had access."

Roz shook her head. "It's all so wacky."

"So many people hated Wayne," Alden said. "Maybe a bunch of them tried to kill him at the same time."

"Maybe it was a race to see who could kill him first."

"Hmph." Alden massaged his temple again.

"Did those mean widdle kids hurt you?" Roz teased.

"Yes, they hurt me! The girl put a jump rope around my neck for 'reins' that almost choked me, and Mateo decided he needed to beat me because I was a bad horse. Future serial killer right there."

Roz laughed out loud. "Nicole did say they'd had a lot of sugar. Maybe it's too soon to judge."

"Maybe," Alden acknowledged. "I think he's at the age when attacking everything is de rigueur."

"Especially reporters."

He snorted. "Especially. Where are we going?"

"We're going to talk to Mae. Nicole said other women in the book club were wannabe screenwriters and under Wayne's spell and probably gave him money. We might get a few more names."

Alden sighed in frustration. "Don't we have enough names already?"

"You mean, are we ever going to finish this story? I have no idea." Roz sounded grim.

"We need to narrow down, not expand. And also figure out why Sebastian seems to have been a target, too. He might still be a target. You're sure Nicole didn't sabotage the plane?"

"I believed her when she described her script, the one Wayne was supposedly interested in," Roz said. "It didn't include an aviation element. And her context has me convinced. She hated Wayne, and I think she still likes her husband."

"*Likes*." Alden couldn't keep the sarcasm out of his voice.

"Loves, probably. That's not what I'm writing about. The Real Housewives of Comet Cove."

"Ha," Alden said.

"I kind of feel for her, honestly. That scumbag Wayne came on to her and asked her to keep it a secret from Sebastian. Her husband. *His* business partner!"

"Sounds like you'd kill him yourself if you had the chance."

"Only if I couldn't get caught." Roz shot him a saucy glance.

He laughed. "That's probably what his killer thought."

"Probably," Roz said. "I'm hung up on what Blake said— about Wayne wanting info for one of the scriptwriters, who was writing about how to sabotage a plane. Maybe one of the writers Mae knows is working on something like that."

"We can try to find out. But we're going to have to talk to Enolia again. You know that."

"I know," Roz said. "I'm dreading it. She's kind of forbidding."

"But she likes publicity. And she doesn't want to come out looking like a shrew. She'll talk to us again." He hoped. "We'll just have to be delicate."

"I don't know if we're that good."

"Not that good!" Alden put a hand over his heart. "You wound me to the quick."

Roz grinned, and he leaned across and kissed her cheek.

A few minutes later, she again parked on Main Street,

pulling into one of the diagonal spaces across the street from Big Bang Books.

"Rock star parking," she said with satisfaction.

"Rock star is right in front," Alden said, unbuckling his seat belt. "I think this is roadie parking."

"Close enough. Let's hope our luck holds when we get inside."

The bookstore's *Hunger Games* door alert whistled as they entered. There were a few browsers, along with the young bookseller wearing eyeglasses with red frames at the front counter. Alden gave her a nod when she looked up, and she quirked her red lips at him and picked up an old-fashioned phone and said a few words. He could guess: *Look out. The press is here.*

Mae emerged a moment later from the back hallway, wearing jeans and a purple Big Bang Books T-shirt spangled in stars and galaxies that showed off her tattoos. "You're back," she said with a smile, but it seemed forced.

"Next time, I swear I'll just be here to buy books," Alden said.

Mae turned to Roz. "How's it going?"

"Fine, fine. You know."

"You survived a plane crash yesterday." Mae's eyes were keen with morbid curiosity. "That has to feel good."

"The survival part felt good," Roz said. "Before that, not so much."

That made Mae chuckle. "Since you're not here to buy books, I assume you're here for a story. The question is, which one?"

"Probably all of them," Alden said.

"Let's go to the back reading nook." Mae gestured for them to follow. "I don't think anyone's there."

She led them to a corner of the store where two dark blue love seats sat perpendicular to each other, facing a wide, square, low table with a display of books at its center—mostly Florida mysteries, Alden noted. He might have to buy one of those next time. He and Roz took one love seat, Mae the other.

"You have a book club that meets here, right?" Roz asked her, digging her notebook out of her bag.

"We have a few, actually." Mae didn't volunteer more.

"I didn't realize that." Roz made a note. "I understand one of them has a subset of writers who get together. Screen-writers?"

"Oh, yeah. They call themselves the Secret Screenwriter Society."

"And now you've outed them. You're in trouble," Alden joked, earning a real smile from Mae. "What's the big secret?"

"Oh, it's not really a secret," she said. "It's just that they all have other jobs or whatever. They're aspiring, I guess is the word."

"How many writers?" Roz asked.

"Why do you want to know again?" Mae asked. Maybe she didn't want to give away all their secrets.

"We're still investigating the death of Wayne Vandershell," Alden said. "We hear he had an eye for writing talent."

A look of distaste crossed Mae's face. "He had an eye for women, anyway. There are five women in the screenwriting group who get together every other week."

Five? Alden inwardly cursed the additional suspects. But he also wanted to know more about Mae's reaction. "Was he a little too friendly?"

Mae looked uncomfortable. Then she sighed. *Here it comes,* Alden thought.

"He was a lech," Mae said. "He was not a good person. But I didn't know that when he asked to sit in one week. They didn't mind after he said he was a producer. And they all seemed to like him a lot. I mean, he had a lot of funny stories about Hollywood, full of people he'd worked with and secret deals. He told them he could make all of their scripts into movies. I guess that's pretty intoxicating."

"Did he ask them for money?" Alden asked.

Mae quirked her mouth. "I don't know. But he asked my aunt for money. Real money. He asked me to put in a good word with her. Imagine that! I didn't trust him. And I didn't want him draining her dry."

Alden kept his voice even. "Because she'd promised you money to fix up the bookstore?"

Mae hesitated. "I admit, I was a little worried about that. But I knew she'd come through. She's family, and we care about each other. Even if she didn't, I could get a loan or something. I was more worried about him not delivering on what he'd promised her. He never showed her a script. It was all talk."

"And we can quote you?" he asked smoothly.

Mae nodded. "Go ahead. He's gone. And I've talked with my aunt. She's OK with me talking about her investment in the store. She thinks it's kind of cool to be associated with a brick-and-mortar bookstore. And it might help my traffic."

Enolia was sharp and knew a marketing opportunity when she saw one, Alden thought. Even if she didn't recognize Wayne for what he was. And Mae didn't sound like someone who'd killed Wayne for money.

Alden took a breath and glanced at Roz.

Roz looked up from scribbling. "Do you ever hear what the screenwriters are working on?"

"Sometimes," Mae said. "If it's a slow night, I'll hang out and listen in. They don't mind. I give them cookies."

"Heck, I might start writing screenplays if cookies are involved," Roz joked. "Was anyone working on a script that involved an airplane? Maybe sabotaging one?"

Alden could see the gears turning, Mae making the connection, realizing the question might have something to do with their plane going down. But all she said was, "One of them is writing a thriller. Kind of an everyman getting caught up in a spy game. There's a big scene where a small plane crashes."

Alden sat up straighter. "Who's writing that?"

Mae looked very interested now. "She writes for the paper. Sheryl Pugh."

chapter
twenty-three

"I DON'T THINK Mae killed anyone," Roz said as they buckled up again in her car. She backed out in a hurry and zoomed down Main Street, eyeing the destination she'd already put into her phone. She couldn't believe one of their own correspondents was now their chief suspect.

"I agree," said Alden. "I think Mae's in the clear. But her aunt Enolia had plenty of reasons to be ticked at Wayne."

"Only if she realized Wayne was a huckster. We're going to see Sheryl first. I hate to think it, but …"

"She sabotaged the airplane." Alden's tone had no trace of his usual humor.

"Maybe she did. I want to find out. I'm hoping she'll be home." Sort of. What if she was a killer?

"The thing is, why would she kill Sebastian?"

Roz couldn't keep the disgust out of her voice. "To help Wayne. So Wayne would inherit the movie studio project and all the money."

Alden grunted. "True love."

"Hardly. Misguided infatuation, more like." Roz reached A1A and turned left.

"Where does she live?" Alden asked.

"Off Lighthouse Road."

"Fancy."

"Not one of the waterfront places. In one of the neighborhoods behind it that backs up to the wildlife preserve." Roz enjoyed the brief elation of soaring over the Star Inlet bridge, marveling at the late afternoon sunlight twinkling on the water. The sky's blue had softened, and the clouds held a hint of peach.

They turned at the next light toward the lighthouse at Stargazer Point, past the grand houses that faced the inlet here, most of them with large boats and larger docks. Roz caught a glimpse of the lighthouse and the sea as they turned south again, then navigated a less exalted neighborhood before parking in front of Sheryl Pugh's house.

It was definitely nice, though not at McMansion scale. It had that modern Florida look, one story but with a taller peaked roof that suggested high ceilings inside. The outside was a pale peach stucco, and the yard was generous.

That's where the place stood out. The landscaping took Roz's breath away: various trees and flowering bushes, crepe myrtle, beds of native wildflowers, and a grapefruit tree laden with big yellow globes, all prettily arranged. A rustic path of flat stones meandered through the half acre.

Sheryl was pruning some rose bushes near her front door, wearing a wide white hat and bright green gardening gloves. She stood as they got out of the car and walked up the twisty walkway.

"Roz! Alden? What are you doing here?" Sheryl smiled and dusted at her faded McKee Gardens T-shirt. "Forgive my mess."

"No one expects you to dress up for gardening," Roz said, keeping an eye on the wicked-looking pruners in Sheryl's hand. "Do you have a minute to talk?"

Sheryl sighed. "Is it about Wayne again?"

"I'm afraid so," Alden said. He also eyed the pruners as Sheryl tucked them into her gardening belt.

"Why don't we go around back?" Sheryl beckoned, and they followed her around the house and into a lovely backyard. There were islands of plantings and more open grass back here. No swimming pool, always remarkable in a lot of this size in Florida. A couple of big oaks shaded a weathered brick patio dotted with a few simple metal chairs, an empty fire bowl, a couple of small round tables and a freestanding two-person wooden swing.

Sheryl took off her tool belt and set it on a table. She glanced at the swing as they each took a chair. "Wayne and I used to sit in that and enjoy the evenings out here."

"You really miss him?" Roz asked.

Sheryl shrugged. "I do. I've thought about what you said. What you suggested about him. That he might not have been working that hard on making my movie. I don't know. Maybe you're right. But we still had special times, you know?"

Roz gave her a skeptical look. "You're not upset about him taking your money?"

"If that's what he did, it's what he did. It's water under the bridge now, and I'm not getting it back. And I certainly learned some things."

She sure did, Roz thought. Painful lessons.

Alden asked the next question. "Did you feel like it was your job to help him make the movie studio a reality?"

Sheryl gave him a puzzled look. "No. He said I was the

talent, like other writers he was talking to. He said he learned the hard way that writing was not where his talent lay, so he dedicated himself to bringing great stories to the screen. Building a movie studio is definitely not my department. Why do you ask?"

"Did he tell you about the deal he had with Sebastian Esquivel?"

"The developer? Nicole's husband? No. What deal?"

"You didn't know Sebastian was Wayne's partner in the movie studio?" Roz asked.

Sheryl took off her hat and turned it around in her hands. Nerves? "I knew they were friendly. Wayne mentioned they were friends one day when he took me to the airport and showed me around so I could get some good details for my script. He showed me a couple of planes he said belonged to Sebastian Esquivel and a mechanic who works out there. I didn't meet either one of them, though. He showed me Blake Burbage's plane, too. Did you know he and Blake were friends? He knew all the stars." Sheryl's eyes shone with memories.

But she still hadn't implicated herself in the plane crash. If anything, she seemed oblivious, and Roz didn't think Sheryl was that good of an actor.

"Did you find out what you needed to crash the airplane in your script?" Alden asked.

Sheryl's eyes widened. "How did you know about that? Had Wayne told you? He was so helpful. But I didn't get what I needed at the airport. I ended up figuring it out online. The bad guy blocks an air filter in a small plane where no one can see it. Apparently, that'll do it. Oh, my God! You just crashed in a plane, didn't you?" She looked from Roz to Alden and back. And fortunately ignored her tool belt with the sharp gardening implements. "Is that why you're asking? Was the plane—oh no. It wasn't sabotaged, was it?"

Roz just stared at her. Was she really this clueless?

Sheryl clapped a hand to her mouth. Then she slowly lowered it. "That was Sebastian Esquivel's plane, wasn't it? Do you think someone—do you think I tried to crash that plane? You can't possibly! Please tell me it wasn't the air filter." She was getting hysterical.

"Sheryl?" Roz used her most soothing voice. "Sheryl. Calm down, Sheryl."

"But you think I tried to kill you!" she screeched.

"Actually," Alden said, "we thought you tried to kill Sebastian."

Roz gave him a scolding look. But now that it was out there, she turned back to Sheryl. "What do you know about it?"

"I told you, nothing! Wayne was the one who was the expert in airplanes. I mean, he did a lot of research for me. Came up with all kinds of ways to sabotage a plane for my script. I picked the scenario that worked for my plot and found the rest of the details online. He cared about me that much."

Alden leaned forward and spoke in a low tone that made Sheryl freeze. "Or maybe he went to all that trouble to make it look like *you* were the one who sabotaged Sebastian's plane, in case investigators figured out that's what happened."

Roz sucked in a breath. A convincing theory. And it would mean Sheryl wasn't the evil mastermind either.

Sheryl gaped at him. "You think *Wayne* framed me? But that would mean—" She swallowed, unable to finish the sentence.

"That would mean," Roz said, looking at Alden, "that Wayne tried to kill Sebastian."

"But Wayne was murdered before his own murder plot succeeded," Alden replied. "We really need to know what was on that guy's laptop."

"I'll ask Duke."

"Of course you will."

Sheryl interrupted them. "There's no way Wayne would have done something so nefarious. He wasn't that evil!"

Roz turned back to her, speaking in her gentle voice again. "He was evil enough to steal your fifty thousand dollars."

"You don't know that!"

Sheryl sat there under the weight of their gazes, looking like a trapped bunny rabbit. Then she started crying.

Crap. "I'm sorry," Roz said.

"He said he was going to help me!" Sheryl sobbed. "The others, too. I know he was talking to Nicole, but I didn't realize he had a deal with her husband. I think the rest of the writers gave him twelve hundred apiece to get a premium listing on some site that he said would put their IP in front of the right people. That's how he first helped me. He talked a lot about IP."

Roz caught Alden in an eye roll at the jargon for *intellectual property*. Sheryl, her face in her hands, didn't notice.

"The police might end up talking to you again," Roz said. "But I'm glad to hear you weren't trying to kill anyone."

"Of course I wasn't! Who do you think I am?" Sheryl looked up at them, angry now. "I'm a gardener, for goodness' sake!"

"You have a lot of sharp tools in that belt," Alden quipped.

Roz was about to glare at him when, to her surprise, Sheryl hiccuped a laugh. Then she sniffled and wiped away a tear. "I still love him, you know." Her expression turned accusatory. Because it was their fault, after all, that her dream was shattered. "I think you should leave."

"All right." Roz stood. If Sheryl was a liar, she was a darn good actress.

Sheryl didn't say anything as Roz and Alden walked out of her little patch of paradise.

Alden finally spoke as they got into her car. "What do you think? Did Wayne try to kill his partner?"

"I think you're on to something," she said, "but I'm not positive. We need more before we can report this. I'm texting Duke."

"Greeaaat."

Roz snorted and typed out a text to the deputy asking if he had any information on Wayne's laptop, including investment schemes and research on bringing down planes, with a promise to tell him what she knew later. And she asked whether he knew if Wayne had a will.

She put down the phone when she was done and started the car. "That was draining, talking to Sheryl. I don't know how she could still love that guy."

"Love is blind."

"Is that what it is?" Roz turned to him.

"Not always. But it's powerful." Alden's heat-filled gaze focused on her, saying so much more than his words.

Am I in love with Alden?

Probably.

Yes.

But saying it would make things so complicated. Would force her to confront the future. She didn't think she was a scaredy-cat, except when it came to big emotions. She didn't know how to deal with those. Work, she understood.

He'd already told her he loved her. But now wasn't the time for her to get into all those sticky feelings. So all she said was, "Can we really rule out Sheryl?"

"Not entirely, but we can see if your buddy Duke finds anything to implicate her." A corner of his mouth lifted, and the moment passed. "She's a better suspect than the other writers who only coughed up twelve hundred bucks. That's a piddly amount."

"It's not piddly if you're starving in your writer's garret," Roz said.

"You mean your reporter's garret?"

"Same thing," she said as she pulled away from the curb.

"If the other women were anything like Sheryl and Nicole, they weren't starving," Alden said. "They were ripe for the picking. When he got them on the hook with the web listing, he led them on and asked for more."

"The way Sheryl was conned."

"Maybe not exactly the same way," he said. "I think she was a con with benefits."

Roz cringed. "She's in bad shape. I don't like making people cry."

"And if you think that was fun ..."

"What?"

"We still don't know who killed Wayne," he said. "And we really have to talk to Enolia."

Right, she thought. Because Nicole saw Enolia yelling at Wayne behind the bookshop.

"You don't think—" Roz tried to see Enolia as a killer. The ego. The need for prestige.

"I don't know what to think," Alden confessed. "But Wayne seemed to inspire strong emotions in people, especially women."

"Should we get a police escort?"

"Of course not," Alden scoffed. "The pen is mightier than the sword."

"Especially if you blow someone up with one."

"Different kind of pen," he said.

"DO we tell her we're coming over?" Alden asked Roz as she drove toward the beach.

"I don't know." Roz bit her lip.

Alden looked and thought about last night—when they reveled in being alive after their brush with death—and tried not to get distracted. "I think we go for it. It's harder for her to say no when we're parked in front of her gate."

"We could lie in wait for her at Lunaria Lodge tomorrow. She says she plays pickleball on Wednesdays."

"Last resort," Alden said. "I'd like to rule her out before we start going down the list of Secret Screenwriters. And deadline looms."

"Why doesn't Duke just figure this out for us and save us some time?"

"Are you kidding? He's waiting for *us* to do it. He's living for your little love notes."

Roz snickered, and Alden smiled.

They pulled up to Enolia's gate like last time, and Roz pressed the call button on the intercom. There was no response.

"Try again," Alden urged, so she did.

A minute later, a voice came over the speaker. "Yes?"

"Enolia," Alden whispered.

"Ms. Honeywood? It's Roz and Alden from *The Courier-Beacon*," Roz said into the speaker. "Could we talk with you for a couple of minutes? We have some information about Wayne Vandershell that might interest you."

Smart. Alden nodded and gave Roz the "OK" sign.

"All right. I have a few minutes," the writer said.

A moment later, the gate slid open and let them in.

"No Craig," Alden observed as Roz eased up the driveway and parked between the garage and the huge pink house.

"Good. He's a watchdog we don't need."

"More like a lapdog."

Roz quirked her mouth at him as she stopped the car. "He's loyal. Nothing wrong with that."

"Just the same, he tried to get rid of us before. I think it'll be easier without him there. He's probably still writing at the coffee shop."

Enolia opened the door before they even had a chance to ring the doorbell. "Come on in," she said, looking less formal this time in black jeans and a baggy shirt with a glittering gray and white zebra print, her hair pinned up. "Craig is busy, so I'm afraid I have no lemonade today."

"Oh, we're fine," Roz said. "Thanks for taking the time."

"You intrigued me." Enolia led them into the living room, where she curled into her big chair. They sat catty-corner to her, on the couch facing the electric fireplace—currently dark —and the wall of bookshelves. "So. You've learned something about Wayne?"

"A few things," Alden said. "Did you know that he had

promised several writers that he was going to get their work made into movies?"

She looked down and smoothed her shirt when it didn't need smoothing. Then she looked up. "Oh, I knew he had several protégés. He liked to foster young talent. Especially young women." Her smile seemed odd. Hard.

Roz turned to Alden slightly, lifting her eyebrows. *Run with it,* she seemed to say. So he did.

"He asked them for money. I understand he asked you for money, too?"

The corner of Enolia's smile twitched, and then it flattened. "I see Mae has been talking out of turn. Oh, I don't blame her. She's such an open-hearted soul. I suppose his financial records will be prodded and poked by those police people anyway. Yes, I invested some money into the screen adaptations."

"Care to say how much?" Alden asked.

"I don't know exactly. I mean, I know roughly. Perhaps a hundred thousand? I was paying in installments, so he'd only received about half of that. He said I might get credit as a co-producer eventually with a more significant investment. I expected to make it all back and then some. If you can't invest in your own work, what can you invest in?"

"It seems as if Wayne hadn't made much progress on his movie projects." Alden tried to be tactful. "Craig told us Wayne had something lined up at Netflix. In fact, my source there says no adaptations of your books are in the works."

"And are you sure your source is correct?" Enolia sounded smug. "I've been talking with one of their content executives. Reynold Casper. He's very excited."

"Reynold Casper ... he's a friend of Wayne's," Alden said. "He works as a tour guide at Disneyland."

Enolia's smile faltered. Then she swallowed. "Perhaps that's his second job." Even she didn't sound convinced. "Go get Craig for me. He talked to him too. He can show you the books and the correspondence. I'm sure it's all there."

Oh, this was going to hurt. He wasn't sure he wanted to see his favorite author's reaction when she saw the truth.

"Where's Craig?" Roz asked.

"In his apartment above the garage," Enolia said.

"What's in the garage?" Alden asked. Roz shot him a funny look, but he couldn't help himself.

"Cars, you mean? My baby-blue 1968 Mercedes convertible, for one. I love that car. But for more practical driving, there's the Bentley."

That was the practical car? Alden almost wept.

"And there's the Toyota I bought for Craig," Enolia continued. "Upstairs in the apartment, there's a storage room with all my business archives as well. Craig looks after them. I don't like them around me in my office. It hurts my creativity if I think too much about money."

Spoken like someone who had a lot of it. Alden glanced at Roz.

"We'll take a look and sort this all out," Roz said, but her eyes told him she didn't believe her comforting words.

The author seemed genuinely clueless about Wayne's scam. If so, why did she yell at him in the alley behind Big Bang Books?

He'd ask that question when he got back. In the meantime, they were about to get some real juice for the story.

"I'll get Craig." Alden headed for the door. "I'll be right back."

chapter
twenty-five

ROZ ENDURED the awkward silence for about twenty seconds before falling into her own trap. Stay quiet long enough, and your subject wants to fill the silence. In her case, she was bursting with questions.

"How much did Wayne tell you about his business dealings?" Roz asked Enolia.

"He told me what I needed to know. His lawyer was kind enough to draw up the papers I signed that gave Wayne the resources he needed to shop around my books."

Wayne's "kind" lawyer. The same one who set up the sham escrow account with Sebastian Esquivel?

"So if you're confident in the movie deal he was pursuing—"

"I am," Enolia said.

"What were you and Wayne arguing about in the alley before your book signing?"

Enolia sucked in a breath. Paused. "Who told you that?"

"You were seen. What was the fight about?" Roz shifted slightly so she could leap out of the way in case Enolia turned on her. After all, she might still be a crazed killer and could lash out, since she was cornered.

Roz belatedly realized she should've just waited for Alden to come back before confronting Enolia about Wayne.

Enolia's look of shock melted into something calm and crafty. "Tell me, what would you do if you found Alden in bed with another woman?"

"What?" Roz exclaimed.

"You're together, aren't you?"

"I—" There was no use denying it. Were they that obvious? "Yes."

"And?"

"I wouldn't be happy about it," Roz admitted.

"Would you get upset?"

"Of course." And then she realized what Enolia was saying and leaned forward. "You and Wayne were ... together?"

"We had a relationship. I thought it was an exclusive one. And then he set down his phone in a careless moment and walked away just when a particularly lurid text appeared on the screen. I saw it. I picked it up. How could I not? Could you have resisted?"

"I—I don't know." Roz was still trying to figure out just how angry Enolia was. She didn't need disturbing thoughts like that—of Alden with someone else—planted in her head.

"You're a curious person—I mean driven by curiosity," the novelist said. "I think you know the answer. I read the whole chat. His disgusting exchange with that woman. She works at your newspaper, you know."

"Sheryl Pugh? She's a freelancer."

Enolia glared at her. "She's a tramp. Making plans to go away with him. Gushing about how much he was helping her. Commenting on his anatomy."

"Ew." Roz didn't mean to say it, but there was such a thing as too much information.

Enolia nodded in agreement, her eyes bright with emotion. "I'm not saying I was in love with Wayne. But I expected some loyalty. I think the worst part was that he'd lied to me. And I'd had a bad morning. I was nervous about appearing at the bookstore."

"You didn't seem nervous."

"I'm a very good actress. I'm a closet introvert." She acted like she was telling Roz a secret, but Roz got the feeling the line was well-rehearsed. And hard to believe, given how she'd teased her audience. "Besides, I've had one or two obsessive fans cross the line over the years, which adds to my jitters. It's why I like having people I trust around me when I do an event like that—Mae and Craig, who can be a bodyguard when I need him to be. To tell the truth, I usually have a Taser in my bag as well."

So Enolia wasn't afraid to use a little violence. "Had you just found out that Wayne wasn't—loyal?"

"I saw the messages that morning, just before he left my house."

"Why didn't you confront him then?"

"I wasn't ready. My characters often have a snappy comeback. But I'm one of those people who has to think about what to say, especially when I've experienced a shock. I fumed all morning, going over it again and again in my head. I couldn't focus at all before the reading. I realized I couldn't go on unless I set things straight with Wayne. I'd heard his voice in the hall. So I followed him out back. And I told him exactly where he could stuff that phone."

Roz nodded, swallowing a laugh that tried to escape. "Did you hit him?"

A proud glint sparked in Enolia's eyes. "I yelled at him. I told him we were done, though I still expected him to deliver on his business obligations. And I smacked him the way a trifling man ought to be smacked. And then I went inside feeling much better."

"How many times did you hit him?"

Enolia seemed surprised by the question. "Once. That was enough to convey how I felt."

"Did he hit you back?"

"He—" She paused. "No. He seemed to be in shock, honestly. And before you ask, he was very much alive when I left him. And then I did my last-minute touchup in Mae's office before I met my fans. I thought I did rather well, especially given Craig misplaced the book I was going to use. I'm always very careful about annotating the text before something like that, you know?"

The book! Roz had almost forgotten about the beaten-up book. The book with blood on it.

Craig had custody of her book?

Maybe he didn't lose it.

Maybe he hit Wayne with it!

"Did Craig know about your relationship with Wayne?" Roz asked, her spine tingling.

For the first time, Enolia seemed discomfited. "I suppose it couldn't have escaped his notice. The car in the driveway overnight and that sort of thing. He hasn't been happy lately. He warned me about giving Wayne too much money. Though I've always said you have to spend money to make money."

"He's protective of you."

"I suppose he is, the poor thing. He's been such a help to me. Ever since *The Wentletrap*."

But that wasn't the first book they worked on together,

according to him. Or was it? "You found him working at a library?"

Enolia smiled, more relaxed now. "Oh, yes. He couldn't wait to leave that job, but he has the kind of meticulous mind that's perfect for research. He just hadn't found the right thing since he left the FBI's Hazardous Devices School. Not everyone is meant for law enforcement, but he has a delicious mind for mysterious plots. I don't know what I'd do without him."

"Hazardous Devices School?" Roz asked.

"Oh, yes. Haven't you heard of it? That's where people go to learn to be bomb techs."

chapter
twenty-six

ALDEN FELT a little awkward about intruding on Craig's private abode. The poor guy camped above the garage outside a lavish beach house. How did that feel? But he was living rent-free and doing a job he loved. That had to be worth something.

Alden found a side door to the building, on the south wall, and he tried the knob. Open. It led him to the bottom of a staircase. In front of him was another door, probably into the three-car garage—he'd love to check out Enolia's wheels. But that wasn't why he was here.

"Enolia?" came Craig's voice from above.

"It's Alden Knox. Enolia sent me over from the house."

There was a long pause. Then Craig called, "Come on up."

The stairs, boxed in by walls, climbed into a nice-size living space. The corner in front of Alden held a kitchenette, with a bistro table and one chair.

He pivoted left at the top where the railing ended and stepped into the room. Farther in was a bigger table topped with a sprawling computer system, books and electronics. A desk chair faced three monitors. From there, the user would have a view out the east-facing windows to Alden's right. They gave the place redeeming light—now tinged with the oranges of sunset—and the tiniest glimpse of the ocean where the view wasn't blocked by Enolia's house.

Cardboard boxes were piled under the table and all over the floor nearby. Every wall sported stuffed bookcases, though the one in the back of the room held a TV as well. So many books. Lots of thrillers, it looked like, mixed with nonfiction.

A simple soft chair sat in front of the TV-bookcase wall. There was an alcove on the left with more doors. It looked like a bathroom, maybe the bedroom and a closed door—possibly the storage room Enolia mentioned. There were earth-tone rugs everywhere hiding most of the wood floor, making it a quiet, snug room.

Craig was still in his button-up shirt, open at the collar, nice trousers and shoes. Maybe he wanted to look good in case Enolia summoned him, as she was doing now.

"What can I do for you?" Craig asked, adjusting his wire-framed glasses, as Alden walked forward.

"Enolia asked if you could come to the house and bring her business records relating to her agreements with Wayne Vandershell, plus anything you have on her screen projects."

Craig thought about it for a second. "All right. Wayne didn't give us much of the latter, but I have folders I can dig up." He stepped into the alcove and opened the closed door, revealing a small room packed with filing cabinets.

"Is she not big on computers?" Alden asked, wandering to the bookshelves.

Craig had a beautiful collection of Enolia Honeywood first editions next to the TV. Alden idly pulled out *The Wentletrap* hardcover and ran his fingers over the raised design on the slick dust jacket.

Craig's voice was muffled from inside the file room. "It's all on her computer, but she prefers paper copies, and she likes me to take care of the files."

"Because you're indispensable," Alden said, echoing what Craig had told them before. He turned to the title page, where Enolia had signed it.

Craig chuckled. "That's exactly right. Nobody is as good to her as I am."

You're so good to me, Enolia's inscription said. *I hope this is the first of many collaborations. You're the researcher I never knew I needed.* A big, flamboyant signature followed the message.

The Wentletrap. But Craig had told them he didn't work with her until *The Calico Killer*, which Alden was sure came later.

"Here's one." Craig dropped a folder on the cluttered table behind Alden. "I've got one more in another drawer. Hang on." He went back into the storage room.

A bell rang in Alden's memory. He flipped through Enolia Honeywood's book list in his mind.

Wait. He didn't have to flip through the list. He extracted *Conched Out* from the shelf, one of her later books, and opened it to the back until he found her list of titles. It was a long list. He scanned until he saw what he was looking for.

The Wentletrap.
The Lightning Man.
The Calico Killer.
Jingle Shells ...

He paused. *The Lightning Man.* A lightning whelk reference. But more than that. He remembered now. It was about a mad bomber. Very technical. Alden had been impressed by the detail.

He pushed *Conched Out* back onto the shelf, touched the

spines between, counting back down to *The Lightning Man*. He opened the book to the title page and its lavish scrawl.

Craig, your expertise never ceases to amaze me. This was the book you were born to write with me. I'm glad you left the FBI bomb school.
You belong with me!
All my love, Enolia

So much to unpack. Did Craig actually do some of her writing? And how much did he *belong* with her?

More to the point—what the hell did she mean by the FBI school? And why did Craig lie about working on *this* book?

Alden feared he already knew the answer. He just didn't *want* to know. Not when he stood in the man's freaking lair. He eased the book about the bomber back onto the shelf and turned around.

Craig stood there by the worktable looking at him, eerily casual, holding a Walther PPK in one hand. Not quite aimed at Alden. But close.

Alden froze while trying to project a casual interest, as if a lethal weapon hadn't just entered the chat. "James Bond fan?"

Craig looked down at the handgun and back at Alden. "Bond started out with a .38 Colt Police Positive before he picked up the Walther. I like this better."

"Fine if you maintain it well. Unless it's just a collectible." *Please let it be a collectible.*

"Oh, I visit the range regularly. It's in perfect shape." Craig paused, searching Alden's face. "You're a fan of hers, aren't you?"

Alden nodded.

"Know all her books, then?"

"Very well. Interesting inscription in *The Lightning Man*. I thought you said you started helping her with *The Calico Killer*."

"Must've gotten confused. So many books. So many years together."

Alden hesitated. He wasn't sure how he was going to get out of this. But he'd like to know the truth, either way. "It was hard to watch her cozy up to Wayne, wasn't it?"

"Hard?" Craig's laugh was bitter. "She threw herself away on that slimy little man, when I was her muse. That's what she used to call me. Yeah, it was hard to watch. Especially when she threw her money at him, too."

"So you decided to do something about it."

Craig shrugged, the gun carelessly flopping around with the movement. "He was bad news. And lithium batteries explode all the time. I just thought I'd help it along."

"But the vape pen wasn't fast enough for you. Or as sure. So you rigged up his car to blow."

Craig's eyebrows rose, and he smiled. "I wish I could've seen him explode, either way. I've been told I enjoy that sort of thing a little too much."

Alden took a guess. "FBI school?"

"You know about that?" Craig had obviously forgotten the particulars of Enolia's message to him in the book. Though he'd seen Alden looking at the titles, putting it all together. He must've guessed his goose was cooked.

And I've confirmed it, Alden thought. *Why didn't I just play dumb and walk out of here?*

Because he had to know for sure. That was his nature.

"Washing out as a bomb tech was the best thing that ever happened to me," Craig continued, "because I met Enolia."

Alden pressed on, trying not to look at the gun. "Was it you who fought with him in the alley? Or Enolia?"

Craig scowled. "She spoke to him, and he upset her. She came into Mae's office all flustered right before she had to speak. So I went out there to have a word."

"Did you hit him with a book?"

Now Craig really looked surprised. "I happened to have Enolia's book in my hand. It felt really good to hit him with it. It seemed fitting, you know? His nose started bleeding. He just put up his hands, begging me to stop. Didn't even fight back. Coward. I got disgusted and left him alone."

"And the pen exploded."

"Not then, though I knocked it out of his hand."

"Weren't you worried it would explode? Since you'd tampered with it?" Alden wanted all the details. With luck, he would get to write about them.

Craig paused only a moment, then a note of pride crept into his voice. "I was so furious, I wasn't even thinking about the battery when I hit Wayne. I'd tampered with it days before that. Or to be accurate, I swapped his battery with one I'd tinkered with while I waited for my chance. It's amazing how many vulnerabilities they have. A little internal damage, a few copper particles inserted in the right spot, and you have a ticking time bomb—short circuit, thermal reaction, boom. I was starting to think it would never happen until it did."

And the forensics team had spotted the tampering. Amazing.

Craig smiled, remembering. "I was lucky, really, that I wasn't injured by my own handiwork. It must have exploded after I went back inside. Maybe when he tried to smoke it. The bookstore was so loud, nobody heard it. It was perfect."

"Did you take the book with you?"

"I dumped the book in the recycling bin—is that where you found it? Enolia would've wondered why it was so beaten up. And I didn't realize he'd die right then and someone would go looking." Craig paused. "And now you know everything. So what am I going to do with you?"

Alden kind of wished he didn't know anything. "You could let me leave, nice and quiet. I'm not the police."

"No, but you know the police, don't you? You and your friend Ms. Melander. I saw you two arrive. And of course, you'll want to write about me, if what you do can be called writing."

Zing! And on top of the insult, now Craig was talking about Roz. Alden didn't like that at all.

"The vape pen could be written off as, I don't know, vandalism," Alden suggested, trying not to sound desperate. "A prank. And the car didn't explode. I doubt you'll get charged with much."

His lie didn't convince Craig, who shook his head. "I can't let Enolia suffer for what I've done. The embarrassment. I have a real opportunity here to deflect attention. And a chance to inspire her one more time. And since I'd really rather you didn't write about all the details, I think maybe the best thing is to take you with me. The question is, how do you want to go? Bullet first? Or do you want to feel the burn?"

What in the cockleshells is he talking about? Alden looked around, his skin going cold and prickly. Craig stood by the worktable, between Alden and the stairs. And given the deranged look in his eyes, talking Craig out of whatever he was planning seemed like a long shot.

A poor metaphor. Alden was trying *not* to get shot.

"What do you mean, feel the burn?" Alden asked.

Craig looked around his mildly messy apartment with satisfaction. At all the boxes. "I had a little C-4 left over. And I've always been good at wiring things. I've read a lot of thrillers, seen a lot of TV and movies. Why not do it in real life?"

"Do what?"

"Go out with a bang. Enolia doesn't want me anymore. I've been working on this for weeks. I'm dying to execute my exit plan." He made an amused sound, a weird whimpery laugh. "Dying."

Alden took in the boxes all around them and swallowed. "Are you saying all these boxes are filled with explosives?"

Craig smiled. "Don't be silly. That would be overkill. Let's just say what I have is well-distributed."

Alden quelled a creeping panic and looked around for some evidence Craig was telling the truth. That's when he saw the yellow wires, here and there, in spots where the rugs weren't covering the floor. He had no idea just how much explosive there was, but Craig seemed to think it was enough to go bye-bye.

"Or," Craig continued, "since you lack enthusiasm, and I don't want you interfering, I'm inclined to show mercy. End you fast. I'm a pretty good shot, and I can't miss at this range." He moved behind his computer, tapped a few keys with one hand while casually holding the gun in the other. An old-fashioned red spinner light leapt to life on the worktable, flashing its blood-red glow around the space, round and round and round. "That's the one-minute warning. What'll it be?"

Craig stood there, no more than five feet away, regarding Alden as a scientist might look at a grain of sand through a microscope—as if he were mildly interesting but not particularly important.

I have to do something. Now.

Then Alden caught a glimpse of movement in the well of the staircase, behind Craig.

Alden kept his gaze focused on the unhinged assistant while counting down in his head. "Can you stop it?"

"I could, but why would I?"

Alden took a step toward the desk.

"Oh no you don't," Craig snapped, lifting the gun into firing position.

Forty-nine ... forty-eight ... forty-seven ...

And that was when Roz stepped up from the stairs at the other end of the room and called, "Craig?"

chapter
twenty-seven

ROZ WASN'T sure she understood what was going on, but when she entered the side door on the lower floor of the garage building, poised to climb to Craig's apartment, she was ready if things went south. Or at least she thought she was ready. Strength in numbers, right? And strength in the device in her hand.

She looked up the stairs. Voices drifted down to her, but she couldn't make out the words. She couldn't see much, just the ceiling of the apartment.

As she crept up the steps, the light abruptly changed, pulsating red. She blinked. Nope, it wasn't just her. It really was flashing red. Craig wasn't holding a rave. And there wasn't an ambulance parked up there. So what was going on?

She stopped just shy of the top and peeked through the short railing, taking in the cluttered apartment and the two men in the middle. Alden's brow scrunched with concern as he faced Craig.

"Can you stop it?" he asked Craig, whose back was to her.

Stop what?

"I could, but why would I?" Craig told him.

This was the guy who went to bomb tech school. Who knew all the ways to kill someone as the researcher for Enolia's books. Roz didn't know what "it" was, but it probably wasn't good. So as Craig snapped again at Alden, she climbed the last couple of steps and called out.

"Craig?"

Craig spun toward Roz.

That's when she saw the gun. And time slowed as several things happened at once, flickering like an old movie, but in red thanks to the po-po-style spinning beacon on the table.

Alden jumped forward and went for Craig's wrist from behind, pushing up the hand holding the gun, and it fired: *BANG!*

A puff of dust drifted down from the ceiling.

As Craig struggled with Alden, Roz ran forward a few steps, lifted Enolia's Taser, aimed and pulled the trigger.

The wires shot forward, punching barbs into Craig's chest.

He stiffened in an instant, and his eyes glazed over. He groaned, dropping the gun. Then he fell, his head slamming into the table on his way down to the floor.

"Get out, Roz!" Alden shouted.

"What? Why?"

"This whole place is going to blow in, like, thirty-five seconds!"

Her heart flipped. "Can you stop it?" The same question he'd asked Craig.

Alden glanced down at the computer. "I don't know how. We've gotta go!"

"Then we have to get him out of here!"

"You're kidding me, right?" Alden gave her a helpless look.

"We can do it." She dropped the Taser, ran to the crumpled

Craig and grabbed one of his arms. The flashing red light added to the surreal sense of danger as Alden grunted—there was a world of disbelief in that grunt—and helped haul Craig to his feet. They manhandled him past the table, dragging him across the floor.

Alden muttered, "Twenty-five ... twenty-four ..."

Roz cursed when she realized what he was doing. Counting down.

Then Alden did the most amazing thing. All in a moment, he yanked Craig's dead weight away from her so the assistant fell to the floor, pulled on both his arms and hoisted him up onto his shoulders in a fireman's carry.

"Run, sweetheart," Alden said, breathing hard, "or we're all dead."

So Roz ran down the stairs ahead of him and looked up as she hit the outside door. Alden was right behind her, huffing as he hauled Craig. She held the door open, and they sprinted across the front lawn through the palms and bushes, past the house, where Enolia stood on the front steps, looking anxious.

"Oh, my. Is Craig all right?" she called.

"GET INSIDE!" Alden screamed. "And get down!"

There was a note of terrified command in his tone that foiled any thought Enolia might have had of questioning him. The door slammed as she ducked inside.

Roz wondered if they should've gone inside, too, but distance seemed more important than negotiating the front door. So they kept running across the yard, trying to get as far as they could and —

BOOM!

The air shattered.

The shockwave literally blew Roz over. It knocked them all

to the ground. Roz gasped for breath. It felt like a giant had boxed her ears.

She looked back in time to see what was left of the garage roof—which had launched upward—crash back down into the wreckage of the garage, whose upper floor had collapsed in on itself. The lower walls were still there, but surely the rubble from above had fallen into the first floor. It was hard to tell, since the remains were shrouded in billowing dark gray clouds of smoke and debris as orange flames twisted against the twilit sky.

"Look out!" Alden shouted as something hit the grass a few feet away.

It took her a second to grasp that objects were plummeting from above—pieces of ceramic roof tile—and thudding into the lawn. She curled up and covered her head as more debris plunked around her. She closed her eyes and hoped, hoped, hoped Alden was OK ... until finally, the noises more or less stopped, except for the crackle of the garage fire and the wail of sirens.

She lifted her head. Only gray ashes and the occasional pink bougainvillea blossom fluttered to earth around them.

Alden sat next to Craig, keeping half an eye on the prone assistant, who seemed unconscious but breathing. The man's glasses had been lost somewhere along the way, and his few remaining hairs stuck up every which way.

"You all right?" Alden asked her.

"I think so. You?"

"More or less."

"What about him?"

"He'll live," he said. "Unfortunately."

Roz sat up, too, and turned at the sound of a fire truck

pulling into the end of the driveway. Enolia must have called and opened the gate.

The house looked OK, maybe a little scarred, the landscaping a little charred. Some of the windows on the corner nearest the garage were broken. Chunks of blackened beams and concrete block littered the ground around the garage. It could've been a lot worse.

Then she remembered her hybrid. She looked to where she'd parked her car. All she could see of it under pieces of debris was dented metal and broken glass. It might as well have tumbled down a cliff.

Now it was worse.

"Roz!" Alden exclaimed. "Please go tell the firefighters that Craig used C-4, OK? I'm not letting him out of my sight."

"Oh my God." Roz jumped up and ran over to the firefighters. They were already suiting up in protective gear, and they listened and briefed her and told her to get as far away from the fire as possible, just in case.

"The fumes could be toxic, but it shouldn't blow up again," she informed Alden after she'd jogged across the big yard back to him. "They told us to stay far away. The wind is blowing the smoke out to sea, but maybe we should move out to the street."

"Poor fish," Alden said. "And what do I do with this guy? I'm not carrying him again."

"Drag him?" Though Alden hauling the sad sack that was Craig had been pretty hot, all things considered.

An ambulance crew entered the gate on foot and made a beeline for them with a stretcher on wheels. Two familiar police officers came in right behind them.

"Duke," Alden said dryly. "My hero." He beckoned over the officers. "Here's your killer. Can you take him off my hands?"

Alden stood to give them access to Craig, who groaned. "He basically admitted everything," Alden said. "And he tried to kill me. And he almost killed Roz."

Duke gave them both a look, as if to ask if they were sure, then nodded to Deputy Byrd. She secured Craig's wrists before she let the medics roll him away.

"There's an ambulance on the street," she said. "You two OK?"

"Super," Alden replied as they all walked toward the gate together. "But I'm just so sad."

Roz gave him a sharp look as Duke asked, "Why?"

He gestured toward what was left of the garage. The flames were almost under control. "The Bentley." He looked like he might actually shed a tear. "And the Mercedes!"

"I don't want to hear it," Roz said. "My car is toast!"

Alden stopped, looked around, and spotted the wreckage. "Oh, no. I'm sorry, Roz."

She sighed. "It's OK. We're still alive."

"You two are testing your luck this week," Deputy Byrd said. "We're going to need the whole story."

"That's right," Duke said. "'Basically admitted everything' isn't enough."

"He indicated he sabotaged Wayne Vandershell's vape pen," Alden said, "and wired his car to explode."

"Did you record it?" Duke asked.

Alden shook his head. "Not this time."

"One more thing," Roz interjected. "We think Wayne Vandershell tried to kill Sebastian. He stood to inherit all the money for the movie studio project and get the property for a song. I bet you'll find evidence on his laptop."

"We took a look at his laptop," Deputy Byrd said. "There

was a bunch of stuff in a folder labeled 'script research' about sabotaging small planes, particularly a Cessna 172."

"Was using the wrong fuel one of the ways?" Roz asked.

"He'd highlighted that one," Deputy Byrd replied. "We'll have to talk to the NTSB. One of our people is looking at his financials."

"And you're going to want to talk to Enolia Honeywood," Roz told them.

"After you beat the details out of Craig," Alden added. "I can help with that if you want."

Duke smirked. "We won't beat him. But we'll get it out of him."

They passed through the gate. As they stood on the sidewalk, drivers slowed to gape and shoot videos—which reminded Roz to get a few shots of the fire with her phone.

She and Alden gave the deputies more details about Wayne and Enolia and the writer's bonkers assistant. How Roz figured Craig's expertise in explosives, and his lies about his background, suggested Alden might be walking into trouble. How Enolia had given Roz her Taser "just in case" when she went to investigate. And why the jealous and angry Craig wanted to kill Wayne.

As darkness fell and the firefighters doused the blaze, Duke retrieved Enolia, walking her out to the sidewalk.

The deputy handed Roz the bag she'd left in the house.

"That's so sweet of you," she said, grateful.

"No problem." Duke smiled.

Alden rolled his eyes.

Enolia seemed flustered. "Is Craig dead?"

"He'll be fine," Alden groused. "He blew up your garage."

Enolia blinked at them. "That's not possible. He wouldn't do that to me."

"Why wouldn't he?" Roz asked as Duke took notes.

"Because he's loyal. And he loves me. Oh, I didn't give him any reason to think I returned his feelings. Perhaps we had the occasional night when we kept each other company, but—that isn't going in the article, is it?" Her eyes widened. This evening's catastrophe must have broken her filter.

Alden shook his head. "I don't know what's going into the article at this point."

"Did you know Craig was behind Wayne's death?" asked Duke. "That's what he told Alden here."

"Impossible!" Enolia exclaimed. "He's a gentle soul. He would never."

"Does that mean *you* killed Mr. Vandershell?" Deputy Byrd asked, mostly just to throw off the diva, Roz thought.

Enolia's mouth opened and closed like that of a goldfish bounced out of her bowl. "Of course not." She squared her shoulders and lowered her voice. "I suppose if Craig told Alden he did it, then he did it. But forgive me if I have trouble imagining my longtime friend being a murderer."

"Friend and collaborator?" Alden asked.

Enolia gave him a keen look. "He is my researcher and a very fine one. I would not call him a collaborator. It's very sweet that he thinks of himself that way. But he's a wretched writer. Poor man."

Fatigue washed over Roz. She looked at Alden.

He seemed to read her mind. "Can we go?" he asked the officers. "We have a story to write."

Duke and Naya Byrd exchanged a glance. She turned to them. "Go ahead. But we'll want to see you first thing in the morning at the station to go over it all in more detail."

"Can't wait," Alden said.

"See you then," Roz added more brightly. She, at least, wanted to stay on good terms with the deputies.

She and Alden walked away from them and stopped where they had a better view of the chaos through the open gate. "One moment." She pulled her real camera out of her bag and took more photos and video of the ruins and first responders. The smoke glowed eerily in the flashing emergency lights, against the backdrop of a purple sky. "How are we going to get home?"

"I've got a guy." Alden pulled his phone from his pocket and tapped the screen. "And my phone still works."

"Despite your best efforts to destroy it and you." Roz pulled out her phone, too. "While you ping Toby, I'm ordering a pizza."

"That's the girl I love." Alden leaned in and kissed her cheek, then pocketed his phone, watching the scene.

Roz finished the order, stowed her gear in her bag and flashed back to that moment when Craig had Alden pinned down with the gun. She'd almost lost him. Again.

She turned to him and tilted her face up to his. An invitation.

His eyes as smoky as the sky, he pulled her close, and she angled her head to drink in his kiss. The heat, the connection helped dissipate the anxiety she hadn't realized still churned in her gut. As they parted, warmth and longing filled her. It was funny how you could be right next to the person you cared about most and still miss them. Still want more of them.

"I'm glad you're OK," she said softly.

Alden ran his fingers through her hair, and bits of dusty debris fell out. "Thanks for saving me. And for ordering pizza."

"Always."

He smiled and put an arm around her. "You're writing this with me, right?"

"I'll tell you what I got from Enolia, but you can write. I'll edit your story tonight. I want you to have this byline," she said.

"No. It's *our* story." He stared her down.

She caved. "All right. But you're the one who got Craig so upset he blew up my car."

"Honey, your car isn't the real victim here. Think of the Bentley!"

twenty-eight

ALDEN BLINKED IN the fluttering sunlight under the palm trees after he and Roz left the Comet Cove Sheriff's Department the next morning. "You'd think they'd have better coffee in there."

"I think crappy coffee is a point of pride for cops."

"I have a mind to do something about that. Butter them up a little. Send them one of those fancy barista machines."

"That's too much," Roz said. "I'll send them a tray of coffees from Bean Me Up and a box of doughnuts from Cosmic Confections."

"That sounds reasonable," he said as they walked down the street toward his car. "They deserve a treat since they got Craig to confess to everything. Which means they don't have to rely on me."

She adjusted her bag on her shoulder. "Too bad Wayne can't confess to his devious dealings. It would make it easier for Sebastian and others to get restitution from his estate. But Duke said it might be possible."

"His only surviving relative is his estranged father, and they don't think there's a will, so maybe the lawyers can make it happen," Alden said. "I can't believe how many writers he was scamming."

And not just in Comet Cove. There were a bunch of online victims, too. The police had dug a lot out of Wayne Vandershell's laptop, including meticulous records of his earnings and how he spent them—on clothes and travel and ways to build up his scam.

"What a snake." Roz sounded angry.

Alden flashed back to the plane crash and winced. "And he almost killed us. But our experience will give the story a very personal spin."

"I don't love it when news stories get personal, but you're right." She paused. "I'm not sure who was worse, Craig or Wayne. I almost feel sorry for Craig, the way Enolia used him."

"Ha. Hard for me to feel sorry for the guy who almost blew us both up."

"You think he was in love with her?" Roz asked.

"Utterly devoted. And I could see how her inscriptions to him in her books would've led him on. Her sleeping with him didn't help. But he was no victim. What if that car bomb had exploded on Main Street?"

"I know. What he did is awful. But I kind of see why he lost it."

Alden could see it, too, but he wasn't forgiving Craig anytime soon. "So what's our deadline?"

"John wants us to update the breaking news story online as quickly as possible, then turn around a more detailed chunky news feature for Friday's print edition. Plus your Enolia profile." Roz looked over at him. "She's not going to like playing second fiddle to her assistant."

"Maybe not. But I don't think this is how Craig wanted to

be in the spotlight," Alden mused. "Especially since he has to face the consequences."

He unlocked the car and opened the passenger door for Roz, then got in the other side.

She sighed as he pulled out of the small parking lot, heading for their office. "Now I need to buy a car."

"I could just drive you everywhere."

"You'd drive me crazy."

He laughed. "That's my job." He looked over to see her smile.

"It would be fun but impractical. We cover too many different things all over the island."

"I'll help you shop for one. You know I love cars."

"No Bentleys," she said. "Ugh. A car payment. Again. My old car was paid off."

"Insurance should help."

"A little."

"You know ..." He hesitated.

"Yeah?"

"One way to save expenses would be to move in together." Alden gave her a sidelong glance to see her reaction.

She chewed on her lip, staring straight ahead. "I don't know. Having both of us in the same house makes us an easy target for all the people trying to kill us." She looked over at him with a sly smile.

He snorted. "That's not every day."

"Only Mondays and Tuesdays."

"Is it really only Wednesday?" He was debating whether to press her on his suggestion when she spoke.

"I think I'd like that. Moving in together. But I want to buy the car first."

Alden's heart leapt. He pulled into a diagonal space right in front of the *Courier-Beacon* and shut off the car. Rock-star parking. It was his lucky day. He turned to her. "Excellent. We can talk about it."

"But my house, yes? Your apartment is so small."

"I'd love that," he said, surprised at how happy he felt about making an actual commitment. But this was Roz. He wanted to be with her forever. "Unless you want to buy something together."

"One thing at a time, Knox. I don't move that fast."

"Whatever you say, sweetheart." He leaned over and kissed her.

Roz fought a buzz of nerves and excitement as she tried to focus on their story. Moving in with Alden? Yes. Of course. And yes, it was super fast—she hadn't known him that long. But it seemed so right.

If the last two days had taught her anything, it was that she wanted to be with him and couldn't imagine a world without him. Living together would be an adjustment, especially since she hadn't had a roommate since college, but she was good at challenges. And Alden would be so much more than a roommate.

She turned to work and soon was energized by their project. They posted a short story updating the news, then set up camp in the conference room off the bullpen and ordered lunch in: salads from Virgo Veggieverse, which weren't half bad.

Printouts surrounded Alden as he typed up notes on his laptop at the table while Roz stood at the whiteboard, outlining the big article for print.

Then she sat, opened her laptop and called Mae—and learned that not only had Mae's aunt come through with money for the bookstore, but Enolia had heard from someone at Netflix who really did want to develop her books for television.

"And they pooh-pooh the power of the press," Alden quipped when she told him. "That was my source, I'd bet my film noir collection on it."

"I didn't know you had a film noir collection."

"Be grateful I don't collect something bulky, like fiberglass fish or old typewriters."

"I have an old typewriter. But we can stop at one." *We.* Oh, wow. This was really happening.

As Alden got into writing the story, Roz called Sebastian Esquivel.

"I saw the article this morning. Enolia Honeywood's assistant really killed Wayne?" Sebastian asked.

"Ultimately, yes. It was his tampering with the vape pen that made it explode." And that was an image she hoped she could block from her mind soon.

"And Wayne sabotaged my plane?"

"That's what it looks like, though the investigation isn't over, obviously."

"I feel stupid for not seeing through him. Nicki caught on before I did. She guessed that Wayne had promised me he'd produce her script. We had a long talk about it. "

"Don't feel bad. Scam artists know what they're doing," Roz said, pleased the couple were talking. "But having your lawyer look at a contract is always a good idea."

"No kidding."

"Do you mind if we write about Wayne's promises to you?" she asked. "Nicole was very frank with me."

"Go ahead."

Roz blew out a breath. More great details for the story. "Are you doing OK? How's your family?"

"We're good," Sebastian said. "And I have a new investor."

"You ... you do?" Roz pictured another grifter stepping up. "Who?"

"Blake Burbage. He called me this morning. He's decided the best way to manage a comeback is to be the guy who makes the movies happen. And he likes the idea of a movie studio here in Comet Cove. Thinks it'll draw more filmmakers. So we're going to work together. We're hoping to have at least one soundstage ready to go by the end of summer."

"Cool. Is that for public consumption?"

"Sure," Sebastian said. "We want to spread the word."

"Great. Thanks. Keep in touch!"

"Will do." He ended the call.

"Do I have to be jealous of Sebastian now too?" Alden joked as she finished typing the details of the call in her laptop.

Roz snickered. "It never hurts to have a friendly source." She filled him in on the Blake Burbage deal.

By the time they'd written and refined the article and sent it to John for review, it was after five.

"And I still have to write the Enolia profile," Alden groaned.

"Do it in the morning while I finish editing everyone else's stuff and start approving pages for the printer."

"John said Wednesday," Alden pointed out.

"That was before this murder story blew up, so to speak. It'll be fine. We'll leave a nice big hole for your sidebar. I mean your feature."

"Wow, you really know how to bruise a man's ego."

She snorted. "Don't worry. *Everyone* is going to want to read that profile."

"Especially because I'll tie it to this wild case. But I'll leave out what she said about her sleeping with Craig. The old Alden would be all over that, but I don't see a need for it here."

"I approve." She tucked her laptop into her bag. "We have plenty of detail about Craig for the crime story. I'm glad Hai caught him in a couple of photos Saturday morning."

"Do we have any of Wayne?"

"There's a head shot from his website, and I sent Sheryl an email asking if she had anything of the both of them we could run in the paper."

Alden's eyebrows rose as he packed up his computer. "After the waterworks yesterday? Did she send you something?"

"She did."

"No way."

"I can't believe it either, but she wants people to know how sweet he was." Roz rolled her eyes. "And we'll quote her saying so. Along with reporting just how much he stole from her and everyone else."

He shook his head. "Some people really like to be famous."

"For all the wrong reasons," Roz replied. "For which I'm very grateful."

They treated themselves to hamburgers at the Doppler Diner for dinner, since they'd had salads for lunch, but they turned down pie for dessert.

"You know what I'm thinking?" Roz asked as she paid the bill.

"Butter pecan at the Milky Way?" he asked. "My treat."

"Done." She smiled, remembering the last time he'd bought her ice cream there. When he'd changed her life.

They strolled down the boardwalk and stood in a short line under a blue awning outside the squat white building. A few minutes later, they had their ice cream and grabbed one of the metal tables on the half-full patio, rearranging the chairs so they both faced Star Inlet. She liked the feel of Alden's arm brushing against hers.

They dug into their cardboard cups (hers filled with butter pecan, his salted chocolate fudge) and soaked up the last orange-Creamsicle rays of the setting sun as it shot its beams down the length of the waterway and toward the ocean. A few small boats slid west, motoring under the bridge toward the lagoon. But one sailboat, its white sail alight with the golden glow, headed toward the sea for a sunset cruise.

The lighthouse on Stargazer Point across the inlet came to life, its bright light winking.

"That's you, you know," Alden said, looking out over the water.

"What?"

"The lighthouse. My beacon. My guiding light. That's as cheesy as my writing gets, by the way."

Her heart skipped a beat. "You should put that in your novel."

"Aw, come on." But he shot her a sidelong grin. "What am I writing, romance?"

"Maybe." She swallowed a buttery spoonful of the ice cream. "All great stories have some romance in them."

"Ours does, for sure." He eyed her with more hesitance this time. Perhaps a little worry. A little doubt?

Life was full of doubt. But she didn't want him to have one second's doubt about them. She set the ice cream cup on the table, dug into her bag for a pen, wrote on her napkin, folded it and handed it to him.

"I wanted you to have this in writing," she said.

He set down his cup and opened the napkin.

I love you, it said.

He looked at her, his eyes twinkling. A corner of his mouth turned up. "I'm not sure this will hold up in court."

"It's iron-clad." Roz placed a hand on his cheek and kissed him, tasting all the sugar and wit and silliness and courage and strength of him as he kissed her back.

When they finished, the sun had slipped below the horizon. But the light was still magical, and the night was still young.

-30-

afterword

Thanks for reading! Roz and Alden will return in *Ink and Infamy*.

Get notified about the next release in my newsletter. Sign up for fun original content, giveaways, news and cocktail recipes, and I'll send you free stories. I also have a Facebook group where readers can hang out and chat about books and life—please join us in Lucy's Lounge. And you can always find me at LucyLakestone.com!

If you enjoyed this mystery, you might also like my Bohemia Bartenders Mysteries. Mixologist Pepper Revelle joins a team of bartenders who travel to events where life is a cocktail of fun, until it's shaken into madcap mayhem ... and murder.

The Bohemia Bartenders Mysteries are funny whodunits with a dash of romance set in a convivial collective of cocktail lovers, eccentrics and mixologists. These quasi-cozy culinary comedies contain a hint of heat, a splash of cursing and shots of laughter, served over hand-carved ice.

The series starts with *Risky Whiskey.*

About the book

Stirring up trouble in New Orleans ...

Eager to shake up her drinks and her life, mixologist Pepper Revelle jumps at an invitation to join the elite Bohemia Bartenders. Leader Neil thinks she'll be the perfect advance gal for his team at a colorful cocktail convention in her hometown of New Orleans, but the job turns out to be more bananas than a drunk monkey. Setting up the key tasting for their distiller client, she and Neil discover their whiskey has gone dangerously bad. But how? And was this shocking poisoning more than an accident?

As Pepper and Neil try to figure out what happened, keep the drinks flowing and help distiller Dash Reynolds survive the weekend, they find themselves the target of increasingly scary attacks. Maybe it's the danger, or maybe it's the drinks, but Pepper also can't help an inconvenient attraction to cocktail nerd Neil as they stir up trouble and try to figure out who's out to get them — before they're sliced and squeezed like a lemon twist in a Sazerac.

All the links: LucyLakestone.com/risky-whiskey/

notes and thanks

A REPORTER'S LIFE is rarely as exciting as Roz and Alden's, unless they're war correspondents, covering disasters, or dealing directly with political upheaval. A local journalist's bread and butter is reporting on government, people and sports, in a mix of facts and features and, at least sometimes, fun.

I take a lighter approach to journalism in the Comet Cove Mysteries, which happen "once upon a time," as I say on page one. I've always been fond of a good comedy, and I enjoy mixing romance and mystery.

I come from a journalism background. I've worked on tiny newspapers, back when paper was the only way to go, as well as medium and large papers. That world has changed so much. But I applaud the hearty journalists who continue to pursue ethical and fair stories in a world that often doesn't want to hear them.

By the way, the "-30-" at the end of the story is the traditional newspaper mark that signified to an editor the end of an article. Its origins are debatable.

Comet Cove is a fictional town with an invented geography, located just south of another fictional town, Bohemia Beach, which plays a role in my hot romances and funny quasi-cozy Bohemia Bartenders Mysteries. The map at the front of the book gives you a general sense of how the inlet cuts through the barrier island from the Atlantic Ocean to the (real) Indian River Lagoon.

I live on the Space Coast, which, like much of eastern Florida, has beach towns located on barrier islands. Their locations make them beautiful, fascinating and vulnerable places. I liked the idea of celebrities discovering one of these charming little towns and all the ripples their invasion would cause in its tranquil life ... and all the stories local reporters might discover.

I'm grateful to several people for helping me get the second book in this series on the page.

Thank you to author and pilot Sandy Parks, who gave me fantastic intel on how a pilot might talk on the radio in situations like the ones in this book. I did a lot of research, too. Any mistakes in the execution are mine.

Thank you to my friends in Florida Star Fiction Writers, which is full of supportive, inspiring authors who are always willing to share what they know. And to the writers of The Office, thank you for that daily dose of sanity and connection.

I appreciate Naomi Bellina for trying to talk me off the edge of the cliff, even if I keep going back there. And thanks to Alethea Kontis for the mini writing retreats and creative conversations during the epic miles on the road in Tornado Alley.

Thanks so much to the eagle-eyed Maggie March for the brilliant beta-read.

A big shout-out to editor Holly Martin. I so appreciate her steadfast support and sharp eye for grammar and the finer things.

Mr. Lakestone, still a voracious newspaper reader, is the best. He encourages my dreams, tolerates my deadlines, and is always willing to hand out my card when I'm fading into the wallpaper.

Lastly, dear reader, thank you for picking up the books, writing reviews, and jumping into my worlds with me. It's great to see you.

Books by Lucy Lakestone

BOHEMIA BARTENDERS MYSTERIES

These funny mysteries star Pepper Revelle and a team of mixologists who travel to colorful events where life is a cocktail of fun — until it's shaken into madcap mayhem ... and murder.

RISKY WHISKEY

BAFFLED BY BITTERS - *story free to subscribers*

WRECKED BY RUM

VEXED BY VODKA

JIGGERED BY GIN

BEGUILED BY BOURBON

SHOCKED BY CHAMPAGNE

WHY OH RYE?

SMOKED BY SCOTCH

BOHEMIA BARTENDERS COCKTAIL COLORING BOOK

COMET COVE MYSTERIES

SCOOP AND SCANDAL

PEN AND PERIL

The **BOHEMIA BEACH** Series

Award-winning hot contemporary romance

In a beautiful small city on Florida's east coast, artists meet, create, laugh and love. Where restless hearts are fueled by secrets and imagination, romance is impossible to resist. Welcome to the seductive tropical escape that's home to drama, humor and lots of heat – Bohemia Beach.

BOHEMIA BEACH

BOHEMIA LIGHT

BOHEMIA BLUES

BOHEMIA HEAT

BOHEMIA NIGHTS

BACK TO BOHEMIA - *story free to subscribers*

BOHEMIA BELLS

BOHEMIA CHILLS

Bohemia Beach Series Boxed Sets:

Books 1-3 | Books 4-7

The **STORM SEEKERS SERIES**

Writing as Chris Kridler

FUNNEL VISION

TORNADO PINBALL

ZAP BANG

Storm Seekers Series Boxed Set: Books 1-3

about the author

Lucy Lakestone writes books that offer fun escapes, whether they're humorous mysteries, hot romances or storm-chasing adventures (as Chris Kridler). She loves sipping a classic cocktail and chasing tornadoes, but not at the same time. An award-winning author and photographer, she's also told stories as a journalist and video producer. She lives on Florida's Space Coast, which inspires many of the colorful settings in her books.

Learn more at LucyLakestone.com

facebook.com/lucylakestone

instagram.com/mslucylakestone

amazon.com/Lucy-Lakestone

bookbub.com/authors/lucy-lakestone

goodreads.com/lucylakestone

bsky.app/profile/lucylakestone.bsky.social

pinterest.com/lucylakestone

threads.com/@mslucylakestone

youtube.com/@lucylakestone